HOT TRIGGERS

HOT TRIGGERS

PAUL EVAN LEHMAN

Originally published under the title "Passion in the Dust."

ISBN-13: 978-1-952138-92-8

Published by
Cutting Edge Books
PO Box 8212
Calabasas, CA 91372
www.cuttingedgebooks.com

CHAPTER ONE

IT WAS BETTER, from his angle, that Bill Serviss didn't come upon the nude girl until afterwards. Because right now he couldn't have given much thought to even her luscious curves.

His pursuers were getting closer, very damned close. And his horse was just about finished, grunting with effort at each agonizing bound. Once more Bill scanned the range for cover of some kind, a rock large enough to shield his body, a dry wash, a tree. But except for the shack on the far side of the basin there was none. That shack was less than half a mile away now, but to Bill the intervening distance yawned as wide and impassable as the Grand Canyon.

A stretch of sand slowed the horse's progress to a series of short, desperate lunges. The two pursuers would gain more ground and would begin shooting soon. They had separated so as to get Bill in a crossfire when they did cut loose, and there just wasn't any chance of his fighting them off unless he could reach the shack.

The horses fought their way through the sand in a silence that was almost uncanny. Bill swerved slightly to the right; he must put the shanty between himself and the two, for if he broke directly for the front door they would pick him off in the brief instant he must take to wrench open the door.

He glanced over his shoulder and saw that the two had veered off with him. The one on his right was the nearest; failing to hold his lead Bill decided to take him first, trusting to drop him before the other could get in a crippling shot.

He came abreast of the shack at last and could see the cluttered space behind it. A pile of rusted tin cans, a stack of wood which might serve as shelter in a pinch, an outhouse with a crooked half moon cut in the door, a well with a windlass and bucket, a galvanized iron tank.

The tank was about six feet long, with rounded ends, two and a half feet wide and about as deep. It was filled to within a few inches of the top with water on the surface of which floated some white foam. Bill headed directly for it, urging his laboring horse with voice and spur.

They started shooting then. The first bullet passed in front of Bill; the second struck the horse just behind the right shoulder and the animal went down like a pole-axed steer. Bill sailed over his head in a long dive, taking his Winchester with him. He landed on his belly in the sand, slid a foot or two, then started scrambling for the tank, skittering over the ground like a lizard. He felt the scratch of a bullet as he squirmed around the end of the tank.

He pivoted and swung the rifle up and around, resting the end of the barrel on the iron side of the tank. The nearest man had raised in the stirrups in the act of dismounting, and Bill got his head in the sights and squeezed the trigger. The fellow went down to stay. A bullet pinged against the tank and suddenly there was a hole in the iron two inches from the bottom. The water spurted out in a stream.

The second horseman had swerved and was racing for the front of the cabin; Bill led him a full foot and fired. The bullet ripped away the front of the rider's hat brim and he reined in so suddenly that the horse squatted. He wheeled the animal on hind legs and sped away, and when Bill sent another slug whistling by his head he cut for the open range and crouched low in the saddle, presenting as little target as he possibly could.

Bill scrambled to the other end of the tank to avoid the water which was pouring from its punctured side and pumped bullets at the fleeing horseman until the Winchester was empty. He squatted on his heels and reloaded the rifle, then moved to the woodpile and seated himself on the chopping block to roll a cigarette.

The silence was deep again. Off to the left the man he had shot lay sprawled on his back. His horse had shied away and was now cropping at the sparse grass over dragging rein. A single heifer calf stood a short distance away, sniffing in the direction of the water tank. The second horseman was still going strong.

Bill heard a watery *glub* followed by a gasp, and sat motionless, his gaze on the water tank. The sound of quick breathing reached him and he dropped cigarette paper and tobacco and reached for his Colt. Somebody was inside the tank!

He rested his elbow on his upper leg, levelled the Colt and said, "All right; come on out!"

There was a moment of utter silence, then a mop of dark, wet ringlets slowly appeared over the rim of the tank, followed by a white forehead and a pair of fear-stricken hazel eyes. Bill blinked, screwed his face into a savage mask and said gruffly, "All the way!"

A pert little nose appeared, slightly freckled, then a pair of red lips, tightly set. A small, rounded white chin, the slim column of a throat, the tops of softly rounded shoulders—

"No!"

The whole lovely apparition disappeared.

Bill got up swiftly, sliding the Colt back into its holster. His eyes were glinting with anticipation and there was a tight smile on his lips. He didn't mind the pool of water now; three quick strides took him to the side of the tank and the frightened eyes of a girl looked up at him. The expression on his face brought the blood to her cheeks. "Please!" she begged.

She sat crouched over in the tank, her arms covering her breasts, her knees pressed tightly together; but even in this awkward position Bill could not help but notice the delicate curves of her, the fresh, soft whiteness of her skin where the clothing had protected it. The soapy water barely covered her outstretched legs, and even as he watched it drained slowly away, exposing the full sweet lines of thigh and calf. And the hugging arms could not entirely hide the swell of the firm young breasts. He bent towards her, his arms extended, and suddenly she drew up her knees, put her dark head against them and started sobbing.

Bill straightened, expelling his breath slowly. He was a hard man, a ruthless man, used to taking what life offered without qualm, or question. Among the offerings had been a fair share of women, and in the process of the taking he had learned that tears and protests were often but the prelude to passion.

He looked down at her and the flame within him leaped. Hell, she was no different from the rest. He said gruffly, "Come on; you can't sit there all day." He leaned over again, slipped his left arm about her bare shoulders and his right one under her knees. The touch of her flesh set him quivering, and her muscles stiffened as his clasp tightened.

When he raised her clear of the tank she began to struggle. She twisted about in his arms, kicking, but she kept her arms pressed against her chest. She bent forward and he felt her teeth bite into the hard flesh of his forearm. The pain was delicious. He said between set jaws, "You little devil! I'll take that out of you!" and strode towards the cabin.

She fought him in earnest, now, modesty completely gone. She struck at him and scratched his face, but he laughed and held her the tighter. He kicked open the back door of the cabin and stepped inside. He was in the kitchen. It was small but very neat and clean; the stove shone, the pots and pans were scrubbed and there were curtains at the windows. He was holding the girl so tightly that she could struggle no longer, and he could hear her painful gasps for breath.

He strode through a doorway into a larger room, half of which was curtained off. He saw two bunks, neatly made up, a deal table with a kerosene lamp standing on a doily, some chairs and a couch. There were rag rugs on the floor and more curtains.

He pushed through an opening in the cloth partition and saw a cot, a bureau and a wash-stand and a chair covered with cretonne. As he started for the cot the girl in his arms gave a long sigh and went limp. Bill put her on the cot and grinned down at her sardonically. *All a part of the game,* he thought.

The sweat was on his forehead, his muscles were rigid and his eyes burned. He put his hand on the firm white skin and found it cold and damp. He said "Hell!" and walked over to the wash-stand. Several flour-sack towels hung on a rack; he took them and returned to the cot. He rubbed the skin vigorously, drying and warming the lovely body. The girl was absolutely lax under his hands. This most certainly was not an act.

When he straightened and tossed the damp towels into a corner there was a faint tinge of color in her cheeks. For another brief moment he stood looking down at her, feasting his eyes on the delicate curves of her body, fighting back the passion in him; then he wrenched his gaze away, snatched up a blanket which lay folded at the foot of the cot and hurriedly spread it over her.

He went out, walking fast. There was a spade leaning against the outhouse and he took it and went over to where the dead man lay. He wasn't a pretty sight, for Bill's bullet had taken off the top of his head. Bill knelt and went through the fellow's pockets, finding nothing of value but a ten-dollar gold piece, three silver dollars and some change. He put the money into his pocket, picked up the legs of the dead man and dragged him fifty feet out on the range. He dug a grave in the sand, rolled the body into it and covered it. He worked hard in an effort to keep the vision of the girl in the shack out of his mind.

He stripped the gear from his dead horse, then caught up the one which had belonged to the dead man, removed saddle and bridle and cinched on his own rig. Then he roped the dead horse, dragged it a short distance and buried it. When he had finished he was sweating, so he got a basin from the bench outside the cabin, filled it at the pump and washed up. The calf muzzled him, bawling for water; Bill emptied the basin, refilled it and left it for the heifer. He dried on a flour sack which hung by the kitchen door and went inside.

The girl was dressed and was seated by the stove drying her hair. It was lovely hair, Bill thought, soft and curly and as black as a crow's wing. The fright was gone from the hazel eyes, but she did not look at him directly, and under his steady regard the blood rose slowly into her cheeks.

He said, "You all right?"

The answer was almost a whisper. "Yes."

"Why didn't you get the devil out of there when you heard us coming?"

"I didn't hear you until it was too late. I'd undressed in the house." She tossed the dark curls slightly and looked at him now, defiantly. "After all, it's only a few steps to the tank and there are no neighbors for miles. I didn't hear a sound and suddenly you came riding around the house. I—I ducked under the water and held my breath as long as I could. Then the shooting started and a bullet went right through the tank. It—it went under my knees." She caught her breath and some of the color left her cheeks. "Why were they shooting at you?"

"Probably because they don't like me. Most cow thieves don't. I'm Bill Serviss and I get paid by the Cattlemen's Association for tracking down rustlers. I was following a fresh trail and these two birds tried to ambush me. My horse smelled them out in time but I had to run for it. One of them won't ambush me again."

"You killed him?"

Bill nodded. "He sort of lost his head in the excitement. But don't worry; I planted him deep enough. Who are you?"

"Pat Larkin. Patricia, that is."

"Where are your folks?"

"There's just my father and my brother, Jimmy. They work out."

"Where?"

She made a vague gesture. “For anybody who needs help. Sometimes they prospect. Or trap wild horses. Please don’t tell them about—about what happened.”

“I won’t. And don’t blush like that; I’ve seen naked women before.”

She said painfully, “You carried me in and—and—”

“And looked at you, and rubbed you dry. And then I put a blanket over you and walked out. I’m still wondering why.”

She stood up and shook the dusky hair out of her eyes. She looked at him directly and there was no fear in her eyes. “Because, Bill Serviss, you’re a gentleman.”

He snorted. “Like hell I am! I wouldn’t want to be one; I’ve known too many of ’em. The lousiest thief and killer I ever tangled with was a gentleman. I’ll show you what kind of a guy I am.”

He reached out suddenly and seized her. He put his arms about her and drew her close to him. She didn’t struggle, but every muscle went taut and the look of fear came back into her eyes. He held her tightly with his left arm so that the warm young body was pressed close to his. With his right hand he tilted her head back. Her lips parted to utter a protest and he pressed his own against them. He kissed her hard.

For a moment she remained rigid, her hands against his chest straining to push him from her; then she gave a soft, despairing sigh and closed her eyes. The rigidity went out of her, the hands no longer strained, the lips were soft and yielding. But she did not return his kiss. For the space of ten heartbeats he held her, then he pushed her from him and turned and went out through the kitchen doorway.

He started for his horse, seeing through a haze of passion. The heifer looked at him with soft eyes, stretched her neck and mooed. Bill picked up a stone and shied it at her violently. “Get the hell out of here!” he grated.

He got on the horse and headed for Pandora.

CHAPTER TWO

PANDORA WAS a fairly large town with a big general store, a few lesser business establishments and the usual quota of saloons and gambling houses. By far the most important of the latter was the Silver Saddle which, freshly painted, stood out among its surroundings of drab, sun-blasted structures like a lily in a patch of ragweed.

If the outside shone, the inside blazed. The bar was of solid mahogany, the hardware nickel plated, the heavy lamps of polished brass. There was an expensive mirror above the back-bar, a thing of such splendor that drunken cowpunchers invariably directed their bullets elsewhere.

One of the factors contributing greatly to the mirror's safety was the fact that it was the pride of Cleve Morley, owner of the Silver Saddle and of quite a few other things. Morley was the big frog in the small puddle which was Pandora and men feared him.

Among Morley's possessions, probably listed on the balance sheet as furniture and fixtures, was a bevy of come-on girls, the most luscious of whom was Gloria Gale. She was, for a wonder, a natural blonde, curvacious, on occasions haughty, when drunk nasty, and, for another wonder, fastidious in her choice of men. Gloria picked her consorts carefully and always had a breadline waiting. She doled out the crumbs sparingly, keeping her subjects hungry. Except Cleve Morley, who had his bread by the loaf.

Another of Morley's assets was the Twin Valleys Ranch, a cattle outfit a dozen or so miles from Pandora, from which he supplied various army posts with beef under a Government contract. The ranch got its name because of a mountain spur which thrust itself right up the middle of what otherwise would have been a wide valley, thus dividing it into two. Morley grazed his cattle on both sides of this spur and his headquarters were at its end so that quick access could be had to either side.

Bill Serviss rode to Pandora and, since Morley was one of the men who had hired him, it was only natural that he should seek the information he wanted at the Silver Saddle. Also, because he was still inflamed with thoughts of the nude beauty of Pat Larkin, it was just as natural that his eyes should find and linger on the blonde Gloria.

Gloria, standing negligently against the bar smoking a cigarette, watched him from beneath long, lowered lashes and immediately placed him in her breadline. Not at the end—there was something hard and virile about him that appealed to the animal side of her nature—but, say, around the middle. Starve him a little, but not enough to sap his vitality. He was talking with Morley and, with the familiarity induced by many favors bestowed, she rubbed out her cigarette, sauntered over to the pair and said, "Introduce me, Cleve."

Her voice was soft and a bit husky and she had a way of observing you through lazy, half-closed eyes over a slightly uptilted chin. Morley looked annoyed for an instant, then said, "Sure. This is Bill Serviss. Bill, meet Gloria Gale."

Gloria noticed the avid gleam in Bill's eyes and decided that this was the time for hauteur. She murmured, "So glad," and extended her fingertips. Bill took them, turned them over in his hand and inspected them intently. "Nicotine stains," he said and dropped the fingers. "You smoke too much, wench." He turned back to Morley. "As I was saying, Cleve, these fellers seem to be roving around without a picket rope and I figured you could give me a line on them. Prospecting and wild horse hunting is a bit too vague."

Gloria forgot her grand manner so far as to let her lower jaw sag; then, realizing that this wasn't at all pretty, she shut her small white teeth with a vicious snap, turned and strode over to the bar. She did not swing her hips, she strode. And when she got there her voice wasn't soft and its huskiness came from anger. She said, "A double whiskey, straight." Bill was temporarily out of the breadline, standing in the remote distance far from its end. Let the rat starve.

The rat at the moment was listening to Cleve Morley and inwardly grinning at Gloria's discomfiture. The wench needed her ears pinned back; who the hell did she think she was? Morley was saying carefully, "I don't know, Serviss. They *have* prospected and they *have* hunted wild horses. Reputations all right so far as I know. And a hell of a pretty girl to look after them, as you probably noticed if you went over there." He was watching Bill keenly.

Bill was thinking, *Another sucker; wonder if he got any farther than I did?* Aloud he said, "Yeah, I dropped in on her. Kinda skinny."

"She is like hell!"

Bill shrugged. "I didn't notice particularly. Asked where her folks were and why, and she gave me that yarn about the prospecting and wild horses."

"Might be a good idea to check up on them. I'd say check up on everybody, even the ranchers who belong to the Cattlemen's Association."

Bill grinned. "I've already started. Spent a day in each of your two valleys. Your foreman turned out the crew and had them bunch the stock so we could take a rough tally. I figured about five thousand on each side of the spur. How much beef are you furnishing the Government?"

"Two thousand head a year."

"Any other deals? Sell any in the open market?"

"No. We figure the normal yearly increase as twenty percent; that lets us fill our Government contracts and no more."

"That's what I figured but I wanted to hear you say it.... Well, I'm going to hunt me up a steak and some hashed-browns. See you later."

He sent a casual glance about the room and let his eyes rest for a moment on Gloria Gale. She was leaning against the bar again and her back was turned to him. It was a nice back. Bill's lips curved faintly as he went out to the street. She was like a puppy who had been too impulsive and had had its ears slapped. She wanted coaxing now.

He wasn't as hungry as he had pretended; he left part of his steak and ate only one helping of potatoes. He waved aside dessert; apple pie wasn't the kind he craved. That Pat Larkin; memory of her remained with him and desire for her clawed at him. What had come over him, to pass up a chance like that? It most certainly wouldn't happen again.

Bill's acquaintance with girls had been limited to the Gloria Gale kind. He knew them and had studied and classified them. Some were like ripe plums, falling submissively into the first extended hand; others were like Gloria, stand-offish, even disdainful at first, deriving a sort of sadistic pleasure in prolonging the chase and surrendering only at their own pleasure. Bold, secretive, frank or sly, Bill thought he had them all tabbed; but Pat Larkin puzzled him. She was a healthy, normal young woman and he was a man and fate had thrown them into a situation that certainly called for something more stimulating than tears and fainting fits.

He muttered an oath, got up and went back to the Silver Saddle.

The place had filled up during his absence and there were the pleasant sounds of mellow voices, clinking glass and ringing coins. His blood leaped when he spotted Gloria, but none of the tingling excitement showed in his face. He let his gaze wander past her as though he had not seen her and fixed it on a vivacious brunette slightly in her cups. The brunette was clinging to the arm of a flannel-shirted miner who was playing the wheel and she yelped with delight when the dealer pushed a pile of chips across the table to him. She drew the grinning miner's head down and kissed him on the mouth, and the fool divided the pile and half of the chips disappeared into some cavity in her dress.

Bill thought, "*That's paying mighty high for a kiss,* and was immediately reminded of another kiss, infinitely sweeter, that he had had for nothing. The memory brought a tight grin and from the corner of his eye he saw Gloria flash the brunette a spiteful look. She thought Bill was smiling at her.

Bill sauntered to the bar, bought a bottle of whiskey and carried it, together with a glass, to a table. He sat down, pushed his hat back on his head and glanced indifferently about him. Gloria came sauntering down the aisle between games and tables, her hips swinging, her eyes upon him. Bill became absorbed in the contemplation of a semi-nude picture on an old calendar and appeared not to have seen her. She turned and walked back.

Texas Tom, a gunman of some repute, ever in the breadline but never reaching the top, slouched up beside her and slipped an arm about her waist. She glanced up at him more annoyed than surprised, and he grinned down into her face. "How about a li'l kiss, honey?" he begged.

She slapped him smartly and he stepped back a pace, scowling and fingering his cheek. Instantly, she laughed. "That's the kind of kisses I hand out, Texas. Want another?"

The scowl changed to the reproachful look of a whipped cur. "Aw, Gloria, that ain't no way to treat a feller." He slouched away, shaking his head in the baffled manner of a kid who has spied a cookie jar on a high shelf with no stepladder handy.

Gloria's gaze went back to Bill's table. He was watching her now and there was the hint of a scornful smile on his lips. Leisurely, he shifted his gaze, glancing indifferently about the room. Bill was playing it carefully.

A slow flush rose in Gloria's cheeks; she was so used to easy conquests that this man's failure to notice her charms irked and angered her. Once more she approached him, putting into her walk every bit of seductive movement of which she was capable. She stopped at his table, stood for a moment looking intently down at him. She sat down abruptly and put her elbows on the table.

"You don't like me, do you?" she accused.

He looked her over carefully, apparently without interest. "Why should I? I don't even know you."

"You don't know what you've missed."

He shrugged. "I reckon I do. You girls are all the same—out for the good old dough. Never do anything for the fun of it, always counting the profit. Anywhere from two bits to two bucks. That's the only difference in you, the difference between two bits and two bucks. I'd put you somewhere in the middle. Say a buck. Right?"

Increasing anger seized her. This man evidently had his own breadline and damned if she'd be in it unless it were at the top. "Wrong!" she snapped. "Not one buck, or two, or even five or ten. No man can buy me."

His eyebrows lifted. "Honest? They ought to put you in a museum."

Her cheeks were hot and her eyes sparkled. "I think you'd look better in one yourself! Bill Serviss, the man of stone. A five-cent cigar to the lady who can make him melt!"

"I've been melted so often that the heat has tempered me. Now it really takes something to make me wilt."

"Indeed?" Forgetting her lesson, she was haughty again. Her chin went up and she surveyed him along a very nicely shaped nose.

For once he showed emotion, but the emotion was that of disgust. "For God's sake cut out the highbrow stuff! It's as phoney as that blonde hair."

That really got her. Her face hardened. “Listen, brother, that color is natural. See?” She bent over the table, parting the golden strands to expose the white scalp. “If it was dyed the roots would be dark. They aren't.”

He bent over to inspect, probing with a tentative finger. “Hm-m. No insects. Not even dandruff. Remarkable!”

Her head came up, the angry eyes stabbing at him. “Listen, you bastard! I'm clean! Clean all over! Get it?”

“All but your mouth. It ought to be washed out with soap.” Bill poured a drink from the bottle and downed it. Gloria said sulkily, “How about offering me a drink?”

He indicated the bottle and glass with a nod. “Help yourself.”

She poured herself a drink, swallowed it, poured another. He watched her with cynical amusement. A strange heat not altogether due to alcohol began to kindle in her. These calm, superior men were entirely different when the veneer had been stripped off.

The anger left her face, her muscles relaxed and she let her eyelids droop so that she could observe him through half-closed eyes. “I have the cutest little bedroom I'd like to show you, Bill. Real felt mattress, velvet covers, pink shades on the lamps. Like to see it?”

Bill shook his head. “No dice. I don't go for soft mattresses and velvet covers. I'm an outdoors man. The smell of fresh grass invigorates me. I like to wrap myself in a blanket, stretch out with my feet to the fire and watch the stars winking down at me. And there's always room in the blanket for another.”

Her lips curved scornfully. “A good hotel in town and the poor sap sleeps on the ground!”

“That's right,” he said amiably. “It's good for the soul. You should try it some time.” He pushed back his chair and got up. “Think I'll amble along and commune with nature. Be seein' you.”

He turned away and she said, “Bill!”

"Yeah?" His eyebrows were up.

"Where is this camp of yours?"

"In a grove of trees west of town. By a spring." He sauntered to the doorway, stopped to exchange a few words with Morley, then went out.

Gloria gazed after him, puzzlement in her violet eyes. She didn't understand him; she didn't understand him at all. She had offered him the top position in her breadline and he had refused it. She frowned and reached for the bottle. She took two quick ones, then her chin tightened and the red lips were pressed firmly together. She muttered, "I'll fix him. I'll fetch him begging and yapping."

Bill got on his horse and rode slowly westward. His blood was thumping in his veins and a girl's face was dancing before him. The girl was not a blonde and, realizing it, he swore. Pat Larkin; would he ever forget her?

He off-saddled near the spring, picketed his horse and kindled a fire. He unstrapped his blanket roll and spread the sougans on the ground. Lying down, he tried to compose himself with a cigarette. It was hard. He dozed at last and was behind an iron tank swapping lead with a horse thief while a beautiful brunette bobbed up and down, distracting him.

He awoke, swore and made another cigarette. He got up and replenished the fire, then paced about restlessly. The moon was high and he knew it was after midnight. He swore again, harshly, and stripped down to his underwear. The night air was chill and he crawled between his blankets and lay there smoking a last cigarette. The fire died slowly down.

He saw the dim shape when it emerged from the fringe of trees, reached instinctively for his gun, then relaxed, grinning. The figure came into the circle of light and the moonlight was reflected on blonde hair. She had let it down and it cascaded over her shoulders like a stream of molten gold.

She said, "Bill!"

He faked a start, yawned. "Oh, hello. Pull up a chair and sit down."

She came slowly to where the smouldering embers cast their steady glow. She was wearing a fur coat which covered her from neck to toes, and her feet were encased in blue velvet bedroom slippers.

Slowly, her eyes on him, she dropped the coat. Beneath it was a gossamer nightdress held up by two ribbon straps over her rounded shoulders. Beneath that was nothing but soft flesh and luscious curves. She knelt on the sougans, extended her arms. Her head was tilted back and she was looking at him through drooping lids. Her full lips were parted. Bill sat up and reached for his trousers. "Soon be daylight," he said. "Got to get an early start."

She dived at him, her avid arms going about him and pulling him back.

"Bill! Goddamit, come here! I want you!"

CHAPTER THREE

SHE STOLE AWAY before dawn, reluctant to leave yet realizing that Morley must not know of her visit to Bill's camp. She was eminently pleased with herself; she had stripped off enough of the veneer to get a glimpse of the force and passion which lay beneath the cold, hard surface of this man and was satisfied that henceforth he would follow at her heel like the rest of them, begging for her favors.

There was a rear entrance to the building which housed the Silver Saddle, a covered stairway leading to living quarters on the second floor. She stole up the steps and into a dark corridor. Outside her door she halted, feeling with gentle fingers along its side. When she had locked the door after her she had taken the precaution of fastening one end of a golden hair to the knob and the other to a tack in the frame; now she found the hair broken and knew that her room had been entered during her absence. Cleve Morley was the only one besides herself who had a key.

For a moment her heart beat faster, for she too feared Morley; then she fought back her panic, unlocked the door and went into the room. The moonlight showed her that he was not waiting there, and she locked the door, slipped out of coat and slippers and got under the velvet covers. She had just composed herself when a key grated in the lock and the door opened. Cleve Morley closed the door behind him and moved quietly to the side of the bed. He said in a harsh whisper, "Where have you been?" He was tense and angry.

She said, "Sit down, darling, and I'll tell you."

"I'll take it standing."

"Aw relax, honey. Come on; sit down. Right here beside me." A white arm came from beneath the covers and she patted the velvet counterpane.

He hesitated a moment, staring down at her, then abruptly seated himself and sat stiffly on the edge of the bed. "Well?"

"I came upstairs early, just after twelve; remember? I had a terrible headache and couldn't sleep. I put on a coat and slippers and went down the stairs. I thought the air would do me good. I went back of the barn and sat down and smoked a cigarette. It was very—invigorating." She frowned mentally, realizing that she was using a word Bill had used. "I leaned against the barn and closed my eyes and fell asleep. I woke up just a few minutes ago and hurried back. I'm sore all over from sitting on the ground."

"And you sat out there from two to four, huh?"

So he had missed her at two o'clock. Or was that a trap question?

"Longer than that, darling. It couldn't have been one when I went out."

Some of the rigidity left him and he put an arm across her and leaned over her. "You sure you're telling me the truth?"

She drew back and her voice sharpened. "Of course I'm telling you the truth. What would I be doing out in the cold for three hours?"

"Cuddling up to Bill Serviss," he said bluntly.

"After the way he treated me!" She was indignant. "Telling me my fingers had nicotine stains on them, treating me as though I was so much trash!"

He laughed softly, convinced. "Lovely trash!" he said, and reached for her.

Bill Serviss got out of his blankets shortly after she left. The hot passion had gone with her and he felt like hell. The thought of Pat Larkin was still with him but now it was subdued. It was her face that haunted him; not as he had seen it when fear was there but later, when she was unconscious, when the features were relaxed. It was a sweet face, an innocent face, framed by dark, softly shining ringlets. The face of a lovely child.

He built up the fire and put on the coffee pot. While it boiled he watered his horse and saddled up, then rolled his sougans and strapped them behind the cantle. He ate a tasteless breakfast, more from force of habit than from any desire for food, and swore at himself for his lack of appetite. He'd have to snap out of it in a hurry. There was much to do. As Morley had suggested, he must check up on every cattleman in the region, even those who belonged to the Association. And most certainly he must check up on Pat's father and brother.

The temptation to ride out there at once was strong, but he put it from him knowing that he was but using duty as an excuse to see Pat again. He cleaned up his camp, poured the remaining coffee on the embers of the fire and rode away as dawn was breaking. The direction he took was not towards the Larkin homestead.

He found the trail he had followed the day before and pressed up into the hills, keeping a wary lookout. He followed the faint path until mid-morning, then topped a ridge and found himself looking into a wide, lush park in which cattle grazed. There were a house and quarters for a crew and corrals and all the appurtenances of a ranch. The trail passed the place at some distance, but he was sure that somewhere a path branched off. He didn't look for it, just angled down the slope and headed for the buildings.

When he neared them they appeared deserted, but there were horses in the corral and when he dismounted before the gallery a man in stocking feet came out, carrying a rifle. He was a tall, lean specimen with a hard face, gimlet eyes and a thin, drooping moustache. He looked Bill over coldly and asked, "Who're you?"

Bill raised his scarf and dabbed at a damp forehead, observing the man closely. "The handle's Bill Serviss. Detective for the Cattlemen's Association. You a member?"

"No, I ain't. And don't tell me you aim to ketch rustlers by goin' around advertisin' that you're lookin' for 'em."

"Why make a secret of it? I come in, a stranger, and start poking around and they'd guess it anyhow. This way the cards are on the table; we play them as they fall until somebody gets nervous and leads the wrong suit."

The man laughed scornfully. "You might start leadin' wrong yourself."

"I might. But they have more in the pot than I have. I'm gambling my life; they're gambling their lives and a nice business. What's your name?"

"Cole Brent. And I don't want no range detective snoopin' around my spread. You ask me what you want to know and I'll tell you."

"Fair enough." Bill sat down on the edge of the gallery and propped his back against a porch pillar. "How many cows you graze?"

"Coupla thousand."

"Any trouble with rustlers?"

"Nope. I got a tough crew. Anybody comes snoopin' around after dark gits a slug in him. No excuse for anybody roamin' around here at night." He looked at Bill as though to say that included Bill.

"That trail up from the basin runs pretty close to your place. Ever hear anything suspicious like, say, a night cattle drive?"

"I mind my business," said Cole Brent flatly. He held the Winchester in the crook of his arm, ready to flip it up instantly.

Bill got up, stretched. "Good idea. Keep minding it." He walked to his horse and mounted. "Be seein' you," he said and rode away. He left Cole Brent standing on the gallery gazing suspiciously after him.

The fellow would bear watching. His location was ideal, he didn't belong to the Association, and he wasn't too far from the border. Also he admitted having a tough crew. He was belligerent, almost too much so; still he might have something on the spread that wouldn't stand investigation.

Bill followed the cattle trail clear to the other side of the hills, saw it branch off and noticed that one fork led towards the border. He made inquiries at the ranches along the way. Yes, the trail was used occasionally, but, so far as anyone seemed to know, only in the daytime. This might mean that the drives were legitimate, or it might mean that the rustlers, having gotten safely this far, had relaxed their vigilance.

He camped at noon, ate sparingly, then rode back towards Pandora, questioning ranchers along the way, getting the lay of the land, sizing up his men and keeping an open mind. Nightfall found him in the vicinity of the Larkin homestead and he gave in to his desire to see Pat again and turned towards it. When he approached he saw horses in the corral, which probably meant that Pat's father and brother were at home.

There was light in the cabin, but he did not pull up at the front, riding through the sand to the back of the place. His approach was silent, and as he dismounted by the kitchen door it opened and Pat flung out a pan of dish water. She did not see him and turned back, but before she could close the door Bill stepped in after her. She turned with a startled gasp and once more he looked into the hazel eyes.

He couldn't help it. He reached out and drew her to him and kissed her on the mouth. She said, "Don't!" and pushed him away, turning her head apprehensively towards the other room. Bill glanced at the doorway and saw a young man standing there. There was a surprised look on his face which changed under Bill's regard to a scowl of anger. He took a step into the kitchen and demanded, "What the hell did you do to my sister?"

Pat stepped quickly between them. "It wasn't anything, Jimmy; really it wasn't. Mr. Serviss is just—impulsive."

"Sure," said Bill. "An old custom of the Serviss family. You're Jimmy Larkin, I take it. Your father home?"

The initiative was taken from him; Jimmy, still scowling, said, "Yes."

"I'd like to see him." Bill brushed past the boy and stepped into the larger room. The first face he saw was that of a man of middle age. It bore the patient, resigned look of one who has become accustomed to tasting defeat. *Pat's father,* concluded Bill and sent his glance to the man who sat by a window. It was Cleve Morley. Cleve said, "Hello, Bill."

Bill nodded to him and looked back at the other. "You're Sam Larkin? I want to talk to you."

"This is Bill Serviss, Sam," said Morley.

Jimmy Larkin said from the doorway, "Dad, I reckon you ought to know—"

Bill whirled, interrupted him. "You too. You're in this. Sit down and listen."

Jimmy gave him an angry glare and then turned his back. In three swift strides Bill was across the room. He seized the young fellow by a shoulder and whirled him around so forcibly that Jimmy came near to losing his balance. "I said to sit down!" snapped Bill.

A hundred and ten pounds of concentrated fury hit Bill. Hands pushed against his chest, forcing him backward a step, and Pat said in a voice that trembled with anger, "You take your hands off my brother!"

Bill glared back at her. "And you go take a jump into a tank of water! I didn't come out here for the ride, and no smooth-cheeked boy is going to tell me where to get off." He transferred the glare to Jimmy. "Do you sit down and listen, or do I have to tie you in a chair?"

Sam Larkin said wearily, "Sit down, Jimmy."

The youngster looked hard at Bill for a moment longer then flung himself into the nearest chair. Bill remained standing, watching both of them. He said, "I've been engaged by the Cattlemen's Association to hunt down the gang that's rustling this range blind. I'm checking up on everybody. You two are missing from home for days at a time; I want to know where you've been for the past month or so. Make it detailed."

"So that's it," said Sam Larkin in the same tired voice. "Jimmy and me work whenever there's work to be had. We help the cowmen at roundup and calf-brandin' time. When there's no work to be had, we prospect or hunt wild hosses."

"Start at the beginning of the month and tell me where you've been every day."

"That's foolish. I could tell you a pack of lies and you couldn't prove different."

"I can try. Start telling 'em."

Larkin shrugged and started his recital. It was a story of prospecting in the nearby hills without much success. Bill said, "Get pencil and paper and draw me a map showing where you've been this past week."

Larkin did so, marking his location and date day by day. Bill thrust it into his pocket without looking at it. "Know anything about this rustling that's been going on?"

"No. It's none of my affair. I don't own any stock."

"Maybe you'd like to," said Bill significantly. "Well, that's all for now. See you later, Cleve."

He strode from the room. Pat Larkin was standing in the kitchen, tense and angry. She followed him to the doorway. She said in a low, vibrant voice, "Yesterday I believed you were a gentleman. I was wrong. You've cheapened me and shamed me before my brother and I hate you for it."

"That's fine and dandy," he told her tightly, and gave her a long, devouring look. "From the first moment I saw you, Pat Larkin, I wanted you. And I'm going to have you. And before I'm through you'll come yapping after me like a lap-dog."

The hazel eyes were blazing. "I'll die first! Now get out of here before Jimmy hears us talking. If he comes out again he'll be carrying a rifle."

"If he is I'll take it from him and break it over his head. Be seein' you—sweetheart."

He stepped into the saddle and headed once more for Pandora.

CHAPTER FOUR

PAT STOOD in the doorway gazing after him, her eyes still bright with anger. Even in the dusk she could not but notice the fine build of him, the wide shoulders and narrow hips, the well-set head, the long strong legs in their leather chaps. There was supreme assurance in the way he sat his saddle and the angle at which he wore his hat, straight and uncompromising and drawn firmly over his crisply curling brown hair.

Vividly, she remembered his face. It wasn't a handsome face like that of Cleve Morley, but it was strong and sharply chiseled with a slightly hawkish nose and thin lips and a firm chin. His eyes were steel blue and looked at you directly and intently, and under their regard one received the impression that they were probing beyond the surface, searching the inner recesses of the mind where secrets were hidden. He was strong and he was ruthless and he was a man used to getting what he wanted. He had told Pat that he wanted her and would have her, and though she tossed her head defiantly at memory of his words she was inwardly uncertain, a bit afraid.

She heard soft footfalls behind her and knew that Cleve Morley had come into the kitchen. She did not turn. In the room beyond she could hear her father and brother talking in low tones. Neither, she knew, would intrude on her and Cleve; her father was afraid of Morley and her brother admired him and stood in awe of his wealth and power. Pat knew that Jimmy's concern over her being kissed had been inspired by the knowledge that it was somebody other than Cleve who had done the kissing.

Jimmy would have welcomed Cleve as a brother-in-law, and her father, a bitter, frustrated man who had never succeeded at anything to which he had turned his hand, would see in an alliance with Morley an end to their poverty.

Hands fell on her shoulders and she could feel Morley's warm breath on her hair. He said softly, "Admiring the scenery, honey? Or is it Bill Serviss?"

She whirled to face him. "That man?"

"He's been bothering you?"

"Of course not. It's just that he's so domineering, so sure of himself. He acts as though he was God. You saw the way he bullied Jimmy."

Morley chuckled. "And I saw the way you clawed back at him. You surprised me; I didn't know you were such a little spitfire. I believe I like you all the more for it."

He had put his hands back on her shoulders and his fingers were moving gently, caressing the flesh under the thin calico. She half-turned, reaching for the door as an excuse to escape, but the grip tightened and he drew her around to face him.

He was a handsome man, tall and immaculate and well mannered. His smooth dark hair was carefully groomed, the small moustache trimmed and waxed at the ends. His face rarely betrayed his emotions, but the dark eyes changed in depth and color with his mood and Pat had learned to read them. Desire for her was in them now.

He said, "Want to watch the stars come out?"

The movements of his fingers on her shoulders made Pat uncomfortable; she said, "I'd like to," and twisted from his grasp. She went outside and Cleve fell in beside her and let his arm fall about her waist. Pat involuntarily stiffened but he did not seem to notice. They walked to the woodpile and he swept off his Stetson and bowed her to a seat on the chopping block, then up-ended a length of log and sat beside her.

He looked slowly about him, his gaze taking in the rusted iron tank, the outhouse with its crooked half moon in the door, the heap of refuse, the untidy woodpile with the weather-beaten bucksaw and axe. He moved an arm in an all-embracing gesture. "Don't you ever get sick of this?"

"Dreadfully."

"You're much too pretty to have to put up with it."

"It's my home."

"It's a dump. You should be living in a mansion, Pat."

"I've dreamed of living in one. Who hasn't?"

"You could make your dreams come true easy enough."

"They will, when Dad and Jimmy make their strike."

He shook his head. "You'll die of old age waiting for that. The hills are full of has-beens and never-will-be's looking for gold. You're just wasting your youth and beauty waiting for a miracle."

Her hands were in her lap; he reached out and took one of them and at the same time slipped his left arm about her and drew her closer. He spoke softly, persuasively. "Come away with me, Pat, and I'll build you a mansion. Build it the way you want it, anywhere you want it within two days' ride of Pandora. I've got to be here most of the time, but I could slip away for a week or so every once in a while. You'd have money, clothes, jewels, servants, everything you need to make you happy."

She observed him gravely. "You aren't by any chance asking me to marry you?"

"Marry? Well, maybe. Later on. I've always believed that a couple should understand each other perfectly before they commit themselves to matrimony. It's so damned permanent."

"I was afraid of that." Pat freed her hand and stood up. "I guess I'd better go in, Cleve. It's dark and Dad and Jimmy'll wonder what became of me."

He rose slowly and once more his hands fell on her shoulders. The dusk was so deep now that she could not read his eyes. He said, "Think it over, honey. Think of Sam and Jimmy. I could do things for them—if you'd cooperate. And this dreary, lonesome life isn't for you. I'd make you happy, teach you to live."

She felt his arms drawing her closer. Pat put her hands on his chest and stiffened her muscles, turning her face away from him. "No, Cleve," she said firmly.

He laughed throatily. "Why not? What's a kiss between friends?"

His strength was greater than hers and her rigid muscles gave under his crushing clasp. She closed her lips firmly and kept her face turned and he had to be content with kissing her on the cheek. Reluctantly he released her and stepped back a pace. She could hear his rapid breathing.

"Think it over, Pat," he said tightly.

"There's nothing to think over, Cleve. I prefer this."

"I don't believe it. A mansion, servants, money, clothes, jewels. You think it over."

He turned and walked towards the corral and Pat stood looking after him. Cleve wanted her, too. But in a sly, slippery way. Not like Bill Serviss. Bill was direct. She must constantly be on guard against both men, but with Bill there would be no fear of ambush or stealth or bribery or sly tricks. Bill was the wolf; Cleve, the weasel. She much preferred dealing with the wolf.

Her cheeks grew warm with the sudden realization of the trend her thoughts had taken. She shook her dark curls impatiently, angrily. How could she form even a mental choice between the two men? Why need she? She was strong and courageous; she could successfully defend herself should the need arise. The thing to do, she decided, was to put both of them firmly out of her mind.

She carried this resolve into the house with her. She kept her mind busy with small tasks and maintained an animated conversation with her father and Jimmy. She measured the windows and figured the cost of material for new curtains. When at last she went to bed she closed her eyes determinedly and mentally recited all the poems she knew until oblivion claimed her.

And then she dreamed of Bill....

Bill, blissfully unaware that he was the subject of anybody's dreams, lost no time in checking up on Sam and Jimmy Larkin. With the penciled map as his guide he sought out the place in the hills where, according to Sam Larkin, father and son had worked the whole of the past week.

He found the mountain stream and the shafts they had dug near its banks; he found the places where their sluice box had been set up; he found the piles of tailings, dirt which had been washed in the search for gold. He did not doubt that Sam and Jimmy had worked here at one time or another.

But, he was equally certain, their work had not been done during the past week. Many signs told him this. Traces of their fires were at least a month old; the tailings had been washed by rain and there had been no rain during the past week; the rust on discarded tincans could not have accumulated in such a short time. Sam Larkin had lied.

Bill, by nature direct, considered going directly to Sam and confronting him with the lie, but finally decided not to do so. It could wait; there was still much to do; and if Sam thought he had got away with it he might become careless. Perhaps more could be gained by simply watching the two.

His feelings towards Pat had nothing to do with his decision. Pat was a person apart, a separate individual, an entirely different problem. He had told her that he wanted her and meant to have her, and that was that. A gentleman, he cynically told himself, would show her consideration, even deference, but he was no gentleman. He had made that plain enough to her. If Sam and Jimmy were rustlers they would pay the penalty, and it would be just Pat's hard luck that they happened to be her father and brother.

He followed the Larkin trail from the workings far enough to see that it led directly to the homestead, then abandoned it. He spent a week probing about in the hills, searching out obscure trails, looking for hidden parks and cattle sign. Every so often he rode to Pandora, and on his way scanned the Larkin homestead to check on the horses in the corral. Sam and Jimmy were evidently staying close to the house. He hadn't expected them to do otherwise; there would naturally be a period of rustling inactivity while he remained in the vicinity.

At the end of the week he rode into Pandora, made his camp by the spring in the grove of trees and walked to the Silver Saddle. He had finished his preliminary work; he had a good idea of the lay of the land and a working knowledge of the trails running from the various ranches into the hills. He had three prime suspects in Cole Brent, Sam Larkin and Jimmy. He would continue to pry, but now his main task was to watch and wait for somebody to make the wrong move.

Bill was an old hand at thief-catching and knew that sooner or later this would happen. The members of the gang would wonder what he was doing, what items of useful information he had picked up; somebody would get anxious or impatient and contact somebody else; the one or ones at the top would be forced to make some move in order to learn whether Bill was on the job or just stalling. He must be ready to detect that move immediately and trace it to its source. Perhaps after a while they would decide that Bill was incompetent or off guard and would try to pull a real steal. He must be ready for that, too.

It was quite late when he entered the Silver Saddle, walked to the bar and ordered a drink. Cleve Morley was standing near him, smoking a cigar. They exchanged greetings and Cleve asked, "Anything new?"

"I checked up on the Larkins. They weren't at the place they said they were for over a month."

"No? If they're not mixed up in the thing, why should they lie?"

"That's just it."

"What are you going to do about it?"

"Wait Just wait." He gave Morley a hard look. "Don't tip them off."

"Why should I? I'm helping pay you for running them down."

"You seem to be right friendly with them."

"I've known them ever since they settled here. I drop in every once in a while."

"The girl?"

"She's free, white, and old enough to know what it's all about."

"Uh-huh." Bill turned his back to the bar and looked indifferently about the room. Gloria Gale was sitting at a table with Texas Tom; her gaze met his, passed on without any hint of recognition. Gloria was being haughty again. Near her, standing at the roulette layout, was the little brunette Bill had noticed before. She had a lanky cowpuncher in tow and was sober. Her hair reminded Bill somehow of Pat Larkin. Bill said, "How much for a little fun with one of your girls?"

"You make your arrangements with the girl."

"The Gloria one included?"

"Naturally. If you can make the grade." Morley's face was impassive.

Bill walked slowly across the floor and stopped at the roulette table. He watched the play for a moment, then glanced towards Gloria. She was leaning back in her chair smiling through half closed eyes at Texas Tom. There was a hungry look on Tom's homely face and he was perspiring. While Bill watched, Gloria shifted position slightly and he caught the gleam of white thigh.

Bill bought five dollars' worth of chips and moved in beside the little brunette. The lanky cowboy was drunk and was playing aimlessly. The brunette looked up at Bill to find him observing her gravely. Their eyes met, Bill's asked a question and hers answered.

Bill pushed his stack of chips in front of the cowboy. "Here, son," he said, "Play these for me, will you? Me and your girl friend are going places." He put his arm about the brunette's waist and drew her away from the table, leaving the cowboy gazing foolishly after them.

Gloria was no longer interested in Texas Tom. Her air of indifference fled and she stiffened in her chair. Bill and the brunette disappeared in the crowd and Gloria stood up to look after them. They halted just inside the back door, where Bill said something to the girl. Gloria caught the eager shake of the dark head and her eyes blazed as the girl took Bill's arm and went outside with him.

Texas Tom came slowly around the table to stand beside Gloria. "What's the matter, honey?" he asked.

She did not look at him. "The little bitch," she said between set teeth. "I'll claw her eyes out for that!"

CHAPTER FIVE

THE CAMP FIRE BURNED cheerily and the two before it gazed steadily at the flames. They were lying on their stomachs on a blanket and they were talking about horses.

Bill was saying, "Your five-gaited horse is all right for show, Maybelle, but he's no good at all for range work. He'll try to change gaits in the brush and gets his feet all tangled up."

The brunette nodded as best she could with her chin resting in cupped hands. "You're right as rain, Bill. And hot-blooded horses are too finicky for range work; you just can't use 'em for cutting out or roping. Give me a homely, short-coupled hammerhead any day."

They had been talking for an hour—cows, calves, horses, ropes and gear. Bill had drawn Maybelle's story from her. She had been born and raised on a ranch and there had been a boy. The boy was killed in a gun fight and after that Maybelle hadn't cared. She went to Chicago in search of a theatrical career and eventually had hit the down trail which led her to Cleve Morley's Silver Saddle.

The story, common enough, had somehow touched Bill. This was a girl of his own kind, a girl who, under different circumstances, might have been like Pat Larkin. So when he had spread the blanket by the fire he had said, "Aw, the heck with it. Let's chew the fat." And they had stretched out before the friendly fire and swapped yarns more like brother and sister than customer and dance-hall girl. And they had thoroughly enjoyed it.

Maybelle said reluctantly, "Gosh, Bill, I gotta be goin'. An hour's supposed to be the limit. And Gloria's gonna raise hell. Did you see her face when we walked out?"

"Didn't notice. What of it? You talk like she was the Queen of Sheba."

"She darned near is. She's got Cleve throwed and hogtied."

"But not branded." Bill was thinking of Pat Larkin and Morley's visits to the homestead. "What's more, if she don't tend to her knitting that maverick's going to slip out of her noose."

"Yeah?" Maybelle got up, patted her dark hair into place and straightened her dress. "You mean Pat Larkin?"

"Common knowledge, is it?"

"No. Cleve's mighty slick about it, but I've seen him watchin' Pat when she's in town. He licks his chops every time he looks at her .... Well, cowboy, we'd better get goin'."

They walked back to the Silver Saddle, chatting amiably. Before they entered, he handed her two silver dollars. "That enough?"

"Sure; but you don't have to pay me, Bill. You didn't get your money's worth."

"I got more than my money's worth, Maybelle. It's not often that I get the chance to swap yarns with a real cowhand like yourself, and I know damned well you'd have to cough up yourself if I didn't."

"It'd be worth it, Bill. You sure are a swell man."

"Thanks. That's a lot better than being a gentleman. See you some more, partner."

They went inside and separated at once. Gloria, wandering about and still smoldering, saw them but gave no immediate sign. When Bill sauntered past her she smiled and said, "Hello, Bill," and he answered, "Hello, wench," and continued on to the bar. He had one drink, took a turn around the gambling layouts, then walked back to the camp. He gathered up his sougans, carried them several hundred feet into the trees and made his bed there. He left the camp fire burning.

He awoke some hours later to lie quiet, listening. Somebody was moving about the area where the fire smoldered and he thought he heard his name called in a sharp whisper. He grinned, rolled over to his right side and went back to sleep.

He broke camp the next morning, bought a week's supplies and headed for the basin where the Larkins had their homestead. He made camp in the hills on the eastern side and studied the place through his field glasses. The horses were still in the corral, but he continued to watch. Presently Sam came out the front door and stood for some time gazing about, then went back inside. Sam, Bill concluded, was getting restless.

Shortly afterwards Pat came out and poured some water on a small flower bed. Bill waited around until after noon, then broke camp and rode up the trail which led past Cole Brent's place. A mile or so from the point where the path passed Brent's ranch he pulled off the road, found a suitable spot and camped. He picketed the horse, took his rifle and walked, leaving the trail but following a course which paralleled it.

When he had topped the rise he found a place where he could watch Brent's range and buildings and, after a survey which showed him nothing out of the way, made himself comfortable and waited. It was close to six o'clock when seven men rode into the basin driving some cattle before them. He had not fetched the glasses with him and could not identify the brands at that distance, but he easily recognized one of the men as Cole Brent.

The cattle were driven into a holding corral, the men stripped their horses and six of them went into the bunkhouse. Brent entered the big house and presently Bill saw smoke coming from the chimney and knew that the cattleman was preparing his supper. He considered briefly. He was as courageous as the next one but he wasn't foolish enough to go down there and take a look at the cattle in the corral. If they were Brent's animals he wasn't interested; if they wore somebody else's brand he'd never live to do anything about it. He returned to his camp, built a small fire and cooked his supper. When he had finished, he walked back to his watching place, this time taking the glasses and a small dark lantern. By this time the light was so poor that he was unable to read the brands.

He saw Cole Brent come out of the house with a rifle. Brent sat down in a rawhide chair, leaned the Winchester against the wall within easy reach and sat staring out over the basin, chewing tobacco. Bill counted five men outside the bunkhouse but was unable to locate the sixth. He was still watching when darkness fell, and shortly after Brent and his men were swallowed by the gloom he saw a light appear in the house and another in the crew's quarters.

He waited nearly an hour, then got up from his hiding place, cached the rifle and glasses in the low branches of a tree and started down into the basin on foot. The moon had not come up yet and it was quite dark, but the light in the house served to guide him. While he was still some distance away Bill found a dry wash, dropped into it and lighted the dark lantern. He closed the slide so that no gleam showed, climbed out of the wash and continued towards the buildings. He circled the big house at a safe distance and moved silently towards the corral. He watched the bunkhouse, ready to drop to the ground if one of Brent's men came outside.

He found the corral and started circling it, peering through the bars for sight of one of the penned steers. When he located one lying with its flank towards him and near enough for identification Bill halted and peered intently about him. He could discern nobody outside the bunkhouse. He was in back and to the side of the big house and the rear of the building was in deep gloom; but the light was in a front room and he assumed that Brent would be where the light was. Bill pointed the dark lantern towards the reclining steer and drew back the slide.

A rifle cracked and Bill felt the wind of the bullet as it passed his head. It was very close. He closed the slide, bent low and ran along the corral. The shot had come from the direction of the house; Cole Brent was following his practice of shooting first and asking questions afterward.

Bill threw a glance towards the bunkhouse. The light had been extinguished and vague shadows were slipping through the doorway. He peered into the corral as he ran. The steers were on their feet and as the rifle cracked again they started off at a lumbering trot. Bill halted and opened the slide again, hastily moving the searching ray about. Once more the rifle spoke and then one of the men from the bunkhouse cut loose with a sixgun. Bill swore, closed the slide and ran some more.

He was on the far side of the corral when he saw his chance. The steers, alarmed by the shooting, had trotted as far away from the firing as was possible and now were huddled against the fence. When Bill opened the slide this time the ray fell directly on a brand. The steers broke under the sudden light but Bill had read the brand. It was a TV, the brand of Cleve Morley. At least one of the animals in the corral was not the property of Cole Brent.

This time no shot was fired, but Bill could hear the pound of boots as the cowboys from the bunkhouse came running around the corral. Bill sped on around the bars, planning to head for the ridge and hoping to reach it before one or more of them could saddle up a horse. He had drawn his Colt; the evidence he had just uncovered justified the use of a gun. He was about to straighten out for the run to the ridge when a dim shape erected itself directly in his path and he knew this was the sixth man and that he had been hidden somewhere in anticipation of something like this. Bill swerved as the man's Colt roared and felt the bullet tear at his sleeve. He took off in a long dive.

He struck the Brent cowboy squarely in the middle and heard his grunt as he went down backwards. Bill was atop him when he landed; he raised his gun and brought it down. The heavy barrel struck something solid and the man beneath him went limp. Bill scrambled off him, rose to his feet. Three men were approaching at a run and starlight glinted on their drawn guns.

Bill said, in a hoarse, panting voice that they would not recognize, "I got him!"

They slowed from run to rapid walk, lowering their guns. One of them said, "Nice work, feller."

Another said, "Good thing you spoke, Pete; I was just gettin' ready to cut loose." He raised his voice to a shout. "Hold your fire, Cole! We got him!"

The man went to the body and knelt beside it and a match flicked into flame under his thumbnail. He held the flame over the upturned face, said, "Hell! This is Pete!"

Bill said, "Freeze!" His Colt menaced them. They froze. He said, "Drop your guns and back up."

When they had obeyed, Bill advanced, found each weapon in turn with the toe of his boot and kicked it some distance away. One of them yelled, "Look out, Cole! He foxed us!"

Bill backed away, then turned and ran. Cole had a Winchester and he had only his Colt; he must play the cards as they were dealt him. He kept to low spots in the basin as much as he could, and bullets from the rifle kept kicking up the dirt about him. When he finally reached the ridge he was sweating and panting with exertion. He found his Winchester and started pumping lead back into the basin at the group of riders who were speeding towards him.

They separated quickly, spreading out into a thin line but still coming on. Bill retreated back into the trees and found cover, but although he heard them racing back and forth they did not come near him and finally returned to the basin. Bill went to his camp, rolled up in his blankets and slept.

In the morning he saddled up and rode to the ridge. Looking into the basin, he saw that the holding corral was now empty and there was not a human being in sight. He angled down the slope and headed for the house, keeping a sharp lookout for Cole Brent and his Winchester. He saw nothing and when he hailed the house there was no answer.

He went inside and prowled about, looking through Brent's desk, examining tally books and bills of sale and everything else he could lay his hands on. He found nothing incriminating; hadn't thought he would. He rode out on the range and checked the brands on all the cattle that were convenient. He found nothing but the Candlestick of Cole Brent. Either Brent was absolutely in the clear or was inordinately clever. Bill was inclined to think it was the latter.

He rode back to the little valley in which Sam Larkin had his homestead. Even without the glasses he could see that there was but one horse in the corral. Sam and Jimmy had gone.

Bill rode on to the cabin, rounded it and dismounted in the back. The kitchen door was open, but as he started up the steps he found himself gazing into the muzzle of a Winchester. He looked along its barrel and into the determined eyes of Pat Larkin. She said tightly, "Don't try to come in."

A chill of real fear traveled along his spine, but Bill fixed his hard gaze on her and advanced steadily. The rifle wavered and the determination in her eyes became uncertainty. When he was inside he stopped and said, "Put that thing down; I'm not going to hurt you."

She gave a little despairing sigh and lowered the rifle.

He asked. "Where's your father and brother?"

"I don't know. They rode away last evening. Why do you want them?"

"I don't—yet. If they're rustling, I do. Are they?"

"Certainly not!"

"Which way did they go?"

She motioned with a weary arm. "Up into the hills."

"That's all I want to know. And don't look so scared; I'm not even going to kiss you." He turned and strode away.

Pat came to the doorway and watched as he rode away. She was worried. Although she had denied emphatically that her father and brother were rustling, in her heart she could not be sure. They had not taken her into their confidence and their actions were suspicious. She just didn't know. And with this ruthless man on their trail she was afraid.

CHAPTER SIX

BILL TOOK a course which brought him to the foot of the hills a mile or so north of the Larkin cabin, where he turned southward, following the contour of the land and keeping his eyes open for trails leading into the mountains. He found a path after he had ridden a short distance and dismounted to examine it. He could find no trace of recent travel and continued onward.

He struck another trail a short distance south of the homestead and this time he found two sets of fresh horse tracks. He turned into the path and followed it slowly, stopping occasionally to make sure of the tracks and watching to right and left for a break in the underbrush which would indicate that Sam and Jimmy Larkin had abandoned the trail.

He came finally to a shallow mountain stream and upon examining the opposite bank saw that the horses had not emerged from the water here. He had expected something like this; the Larkins knew he would follow and had taken the necessary precautions. Which way—upstream or down? Bill guessed up and rode along the far bank looking for the place where they had left the creek. It was nearly noon when he came to a high waterfall. If the Larkins had come this far they must leave the water here; but there were no marks on either bank.

Bill swore disgustedly, ate some cold rations and turned back, following the other bank just in case. He found where they had left the water less than a hundred yards from his starting point, but they had emerged on the near bank instead of the far.

He followed the tracks carefully. They led him in a wide half-circle which bisected the original path at a rocky stretch a quarter of a mile from the stream. Bill had halted at this point to look for tracks, but had pressed onward when he had picked them up in some soft mold farther ahead. His face tightened grimly. They were cute, all right; damned cute. He followed the new trail until it curved back to the stream and once more disappeared.

He swore in exasperation. Nothing to do now but examine both banks for heaven knows how far. He rode along the bank to the first crossing point, then down the other bank to where the tracks entered the water. He took to the middle of the stream so that he could watch both banks, but the creek was rocky and at places deep and his progress was painfully slow.

Somewhere around mid-afternoon he found their faint tracks and followed them higher into the hills. The timber thinned and then disappeared altogether, giving way to huge boulders and rocky gullies and a terrain extremely difficult to negotiate. And then he came to a flat with half a dozen ravines debouching upon it and it was a case of shut your eyes and take your choice.

He spent several hours investigating each in turn and found slight traces of somebody's presence in each of them. He guessed that Sam and Jimmy had ridden back and forth, leaving faint prints in all of them in order to confuse him. It was as exasperating as hell.

Bill finally had to make a dry camp, feeding his horse with grain he had fetched along and watering him sparingly from a canteen. He tackled the task anew the next day and finally decided that he would have to trace out each ravine in turn. He set about it with his usual dogged persistence and got absolutely nowhere. He made another guess that the Larkins had wrapped their horses' feet in gunnysacks to avoid the scratch of iron shoes on stone.

And then, when he had been prowling around for two days, it rained. It was a regular deluge and the water came roaring down the washes in torrents and he was forced to take to higher land. He huddled up in his slicker beneath an outcropping of rock and smoked a damp cigarette. After such a downpour his chance of picking up even a vagrant print was absolute zero. He spent two more days wandering about at random, then started back for Pandora cursing all Larkins, Pat included.

He made his camp in the usual place and ate his supper at a restaurant, filling up on steak and hashed-browns and dried-apple pie. The meal put him in a more amiable frame of mind and he felt almost cheerful when he went into the Silver Saddle. His agreeable mood was not to last.

Cleve Morley was at the bar in his usual place, with the usual cigar between his thin lips. Bill saw the frown which came over Cleve's face when he entered, and went directly to him.

"Where the hell have you been?" demanded Morley.

"Trying to run down a pair of Larkins. They hit for the hills and were mighty cute about covering their trail, which makes me all the more anxious to find them. What's eating you?"

"It's not me; it's Ed Thayer. He's fit to be tied. Somebody rustled fifty head of prime steers last night or the night before."

Away went Bill's cheerful mood. Ed Thayer had a ranch in the same valley with Morley and used a combined ET brand. Bill asked, "How's he so sure of the time?"

"Because he turned them into a topping-off pasture just two days ago. A line rider noticed they were gone this morning and Ed sent his crew fanning out into the hills right away. But all those paths are used by cattle that wander up into the mountain parks to graze and the rustlers probably split the bunch and used three or four different trails. They didn't get anywhere and Ed rode in this afternoon looking for you."

Bill swore. "I'd give plenty to know where the Larkins are right now. My hunch says that they're driving a bunch of ET cows." He turned to the bartender. "Pour me a quick one, then I'll be riding."

"Thayer's probably still in town if you want to see him."

"Seeing him won't do any good. I'm going to check on Cole Brent. Whoever rustled those cows are probably still on the trail with them." He downed the liquor, said, "Be seein' you," and strode from the room.

He didn't glance at Gloria or even at Maybelle; he was too mad to be bothered with women. Somebody had made a monkey of him and he didn't like it. Instead of becoming panicky at his waiting tactics they had turned bold. Well, from here on the waiting was out; he'd start stirring things up and flush them into the open that way.

It was still daylight when he left Pandora, but although he rode hard, darkness had fallen by the time he reached the ridge overlooking the Candlestick of Cole Brent. He did not attempt stealth, but rode directly into the basin, and when he saw the ranch house door open and the lanky figure of Cole Brent slide through the opening with Winchester in hand, he drew down to a walk and called, "It's Serviss, Brent. I want to talk to you."

He swung off his horse in front of the gallery and could just discern Brent's shape in the shadows at one side of the doorway. The light from within fell on Bill and he kept his hands in sight.

"Make it quick," said Brent. "I don't like even lawmen roamin' over my spread at night."

"You're telling me? I ought to pin your ears back for shooting at me last week; but then you didn't know who it was."

"The hell I didn't! If there'd been just a little moon you'd been layin' out there lookin' at it and not seein' it. I warned you I don't stand for nobody prowlin' around my range at night. Nobody."

"I wanted to look at those steers in your corral. Where'd you pick them up?"

"None of your damned business."

"It's a lot of my damned business. I'm hired to find out who's rustling stock on this range and I'm going to do it. In the last two days whoever it is thumbed their nose at me by running off fifty head of Ed Thayer's steers. I don't like being thumbed at."

Brent snorted. "I'm doin' some thumbin' myself. You range dicks make me sick. You're blind in one eye and can't see outa the other, and if you could you're too damn' dumb to make out what's right under your nose."

"I figure to change your mind before I get through. What I want to know now is whether you've missed any stock."

"No, I ain't."

"How about your crew?"

"If they'd found any Candlestick cows missin' they'd report it to me. But you can ask them if you've a mind to."

"I'll call you on that."

"All right." Brent came down off the steps, still carrying his rifle." Bunkhouse is in back. Or maybe you know?"

"I know. How's Pete?"

"Pete's got a thick head but a thin skin. He'll take you apart if he gets the chance."

"He had his chance the other night. He shot at me from ten feet and missed."

They walked around the house and Bill saw light in the bunkhouse. He was aware of a feeling of disappointment. If Brent's crew had done the rustling they would hardly have disposed of the cattle and returned this soon. Of course, they could have passed the stolen animals on to another bunch, in which case their presence here would not be proof of their innocence.

When Brent opened the bunkhouse door, Bill swiftly counted noses. All six men were present, and Bill guessed that the one who scowled at him when he stepped inside must be Pete.

Brent asked, "Anybody notice any Candlestick cows missin'?"

They exchanged glances and shook their heads.

"*Mister* Serviss here tells me that Ed Thayer lost fifty head. Bein' such a kind-hearted cuss he rode right over to find out if we'd been rustled too. He's mighty interested in us, seems like."

"Mighty interested," agreed Bill grimly. "So glad to find everything snug and cozy on the Candlestick. Thanks, Brent. I'll be riding. If I don't stay on the job Thayer might get mad at me. Or madder."

He turned his back and went out and Brent followed him to his horse. As he mounted Brent said, "Satisfied?"

"That none of your cows are missing? Oh, yes."

"Go to hell," said Brent. "And don't come back."

"I'll be hauntin' you," said Bill, and rode away.

His visit had netted him not a thing and had only made him madder. As a suspect, Cole Brent stood out like a black eye, yet Bill had nothing on him except that TV steer. If Brent had stolen Thayer's stock he had promptly passed them on to somebody else. Sam and Jim Larkin? Two men couldn't handle fifty cows in the hills. Who else?

He rode swiftly back to Pandora and dismounted before the Silver Dollar. It was late, but the place was going full blast. Cleve Morley sat at a table with Gloria Gale and as Bill was about to pass he asked, "Any luck?"

"No. All present and accounted for."

Gloria said, "Hello, Bill."

"Hello, wench."

She said angrily, "Don't you call me that!"

"That's a pet name compared with some of the others I know." He gave her a sour grin and walked on. Maybelle was standing alone at the bar and he went over to her. She stared at him stonily. He said, "What's eating you, cow gal?"

Her face did not soften. "Better keep away, Bill, Gloria's out to get my scalp if I walk out with you again."

"Yeah? Well, you're hired to collect commissions on whiskey; she can't kick if we hoist elbows." He turned to a bartender and held up two fingers.

They took their glasses to a table and when they were seated Bill said: "You don't mean to tell me that you're scared of the Gloria gal?"

"Yes. I'm more scared of her than I am of a rattler. She'd knife me in the back without even blinkin'."

"Bloodthirsty little wretch, isn't she? Listen, Maybelle. You hate rustlers as much as I do, and right now a bunch of them is giving me the royal merry-go-round. I don't like it. Somebody stole fifty of Ed Thayer's steers and they're still with them. You know everybody who hangs out at this joint; take a look around and tell me who's been missing the last couple nights."

"Well, there's Texas Tom. He sticks to Gloria like flypaper but he ain't here tonight and he wasn't here last night. The same for Swat Harrington and Harvey Short."

"Hm-m. Anybody else?"

"None that I can think of right now. But wait! Come to think of it Pink Paradine hasn't been around for the last couple days."

"The town marshal?"

"Yes. You know—little, pink-faced gunslinger."

"Know where they're supposed to have gone?"

"No. But Cleve might be able to tell you."

"Thanks, pardner." Bill raised his glass, said, "Here's how!" and they drank. Bill got up. "Wish we could have another powwow. Talking with you is good for me. But I don't want you to get in bad with the head man and his—mistress? No, that's not strong enough. Anyhow, let me know if she bothers you. I think I'd enjoy wringing her neck. I never wrung a gal's neck and the idea fascinates me. Be seein' you!"

He went to where Cleve and Gloria were seated, draped his long form over Gloria's chair and spoke over her shoulder to Cleve. "I see you have the field to yourself tonight. What'd you do—toss Texas Tom into the clink?"

"No. He and a couple of the boys went on a prospectin' trip. They dig some gold, come to town and squander it, then go out and look for more."

"Uh-huh," said Bill carelessly. He ruffled Gloria's carefully piled hair. "Be nice to him, wench."

"Go to hell!" she snapped.

"Too crowded. Me, I like the wide-open spaces." He grinned at Morley and went out.

The grin was a trifle tight. He was getting a flock of new ideas and among them might be the one he needed.

CHAPTER SEVEN

BILL LAY AWAKE for some time thinking. Sam and Jim Larkin were missing when Thayer's cattle were stolen, and so were three regular customers of the Silver Saddle and Pandora's town marshal. The absence of the first two could not be satisfactorily explained by Pat, and the picture of three blithe adventurers named Texas Tom, Swat Harrington and Harvey Short on a search for gold did not register with Bill. He hadn't asked if the Pandora marshal had found it necessary to turn to mining also because Gloria was listening. He didn't trust the blonde bombshell any farther than he could toss an eight-room house.

Sam and Jim Larkin, Texas Tom, Swat Harrington, Harvey Short and Pinky Paradine; six men and fifty missing steers. Brent and his six to pick them out of the topping-off pasture and push them into the hills, the valiant prospectors to haze them to their destination. It made sense.

Bill was up early the next morning and rode directly to Thayer's ET ranch. It was not far from Pandora, occupying the wide end of the valley in which Morley's ranch was located. From a rise overlooking it Bill could see the long spur of mountain which divided Morley's range, the ET buildings and corrals clustered at its blunt end, and also for some distance up the twin valleys. Thayer's buildings were at the foot of the rise and Bill found the rancher saddling up. Thayer greeted him sourly.

"About time you showed up, Serviss."

"I've been riding a hunch that may pay off. Anything new?"

"No. My boys are still combin' the hills, but I figure those steers are miles away by now." He made a sweeping gesture. "There are too many trails and all of them used. They likely drove in small bunches and might even have taken two nights for it."

"Let's take a look at that pasture."

They rode to the southeast corner of Thayer's range. A fence across the valley separated his land from that of Cleve Morley and he had also fenced off some forty acres for topping-off pastures. The wire had been cut on Morley's side and tracks made by the stolen steers were almost immediately obliterated by those of the TV animals which had surged into the enclosure.

Bill realized at once the impossibility of trailing the stolen cattle; they might have been driven over any of the dozens of trails leading into the hills from the long stretch of valley. He looked about him, mentally located the trail which ran by Cole Brent's ranch and chose the nearest path leading in its direction. Thayer wished him luck and rode on to join his men.

By mid-morning Bill had reached the main trail, saw that it ran north and south, found fresh tracks going in both directions, and turned south on the natural assumption that the rustled stock would be hurried to the border.

It was noon when he rode once more into the Candlestick basin and saw smoke billowing from the mess shack chimney and also that of the big house. As he approached the latter, Brent came out with his rifle and stood on the gallery scowling. Bill dismounted and climbed the two steps and Brent said, "Aren't we ever goin' to get rid of you?"

"Not until this thing is settled. How about some grub?"

"Come on in," invited Brent reluctantly, and led the way to the kitchen. A pot of stew simmered on the stove and the pleasant odor of coffee was in the air. Brent motioned Bill to a chair at the table and dished out a plateful of the stew. He gave Bill a tin cup and knife and fork and set the coffee pot on the table. He sat down opposite Bill and said gruffly, "Help yourself."

They ate for a while in silence, then Bill said, "Cole, if you're in the clear why don't you come clean? It's the quickest way of getting rid of me."

Cole Brent said, "You're bein' paid by a bunch of nitwits to find out things that they oughta be able to find out themselves. I ain't helpin' pay you and I ain't losin' no stock; why should I stick my nose in the mess?"

"To get rid of me. Satisfy me that you haven't got your nose in the mess and I'll let you alone."

"Whadda you want to know?"

"Most of all, who's doing this rustling. I don't expect you to tell me that. If it's you, you'd naturally keep your mouth shut; if it isn't, and you knew who it is, I think you're the kind of jigger who'd swoop down on the bunch some dark night and make it unnecessary to bother with guards and line riders from there on."

Brent stared hard at him. "You ain't so dumb as I thought you was, Serviss. What else you want to know?"

"What you were doing with a TV steer in your corral that night."

"You seen that TV?"

"Yes. Were the others wearing the same brand?"

"Two of 'em. The others were ET's. We keep our stuff pretty well down in the basin, hazin' 'em outa the hills every couple weeks. And we comb our herd right often, cuttin' out stuff that don't belong to us. Saves time at roundup and makes it unnecessary for other outfits to have a rep on our spread. We picked them cows up and held them overnight in the corral. In the mornin' we turned 'em back on their own range."

It was a logical enough explanation.

Bill said, "I just followed some fresh tracks from the hills around Thayer's spread. They led to the Candlestick. I'd like to know about them."

"Our own stock," said Brent. "Gathered in the hills and drove back here yesterday."

Also logical, but, like the other, unsupported by proof.

Bill appeared to be satisfied. He nodded and said, "Sounds all right to me. Now just one more thing. You're bound to have some hunches about this rustling. Feel like giving me a lead?"

But at this point Brent balked. "Hunches are jest—hunches. I got all kinda idears and some of them sound right crazy. Mebbe if I told you you'd be more balled up than ever. For one thing, Thayer uses a brand that's too easy to work over. That combined ET could be changed to a Box Cross with three strokes of a runnin' iron."

"And your Candlestick could be changed to a Cinchbuckle with one."

"Sure. Now you know why I ride herd so close."

Bill pushed back his chair, and got up. "Much obliged for the meal and what you've told me. I'll help you clean up and then be on my way."

"I'll do the cleanin'. And you're welcome to the grub and what I told you, even if it won't help you none."

Bill rode away still uncertain about Cole Brent. The man was either perfectly straight or the damndest liar Bill had ever met. He rode back the way he had come but changed course when he descended into the valley and headed for the Morley ranch house. A rider came sweeping around the corrals to meet him and he recognized Morley's foreman, Jigger Malone.

When they had met and exchanged greetings Bill asked, "Did Cole Brent return any TV cows to you within the week?"

"Yeah, he did. Three head that he found when he was lookin' for strays."

"I'm just checking up. Your outfit lose any stock the other night?"

"Wouldn't know without takin' a tally. Thayer had his bunched in that toppin'-off pasture, is why he found out so pronto."

They talked a while, smoking and lounging in their saddles, then Bill rode on. Brent had returned the three TV cows, all right; but if he thought Bill had spotted them in his corral that would be the sensible thing to do. Bill was still stymied and growled an impatient oath.

He headed next for the Larkin homestead, aware of a surge of pleasure at the prospect of seeing Pat again. The thrill he experienced somehow irritated him; why couldn't he get the girl out of his mind? He decided that it was the excitement of the chase which stirred him; he had told Pat that he intended to have her and she had defied him. She would be a luscious prize.

The lone horse was still in the corral; Sam and Jimmy had not returned to the cabin. He rode around to the back and Pat opened the door at his knock. She held her head high and there was defiance in her eyes but this time she not carry the Winchester. "What do you want?" she asked coldly.

His hungry eyes devoured her. She was wearing a starched gingham dress with ruffles at the collar and sleeves and looked very neat and prim.

"You," he said bluntly, and took her into his arms.

She did not resist. Her muscles were flaccid, yielding. He crushed her to him and kissed her dusky hair, her eyes, the passive lips. There was not the slightest response; she was like a rag doll in his arms. The passion in him died and he thrust her roughly from him.

"Damn you! What are you made of—putty?"

She did not answer; just stood there looking at him, and there was scorn in the hazel eyes.

He went on angrily, "You're a supposedly normal human being. You have flesh and blood and bone and muscle. You know what it is to be hungry and cold and angry and glad. When God made you didn't he put just a little desire in you?" His eyes were glinting and the tan of his cheeks had whitened.

She said quietly, "Yes, I'm as much a human being as any of the girls you've known. I'm not a child, and while my mother died years ago one can't live a lifetime among cattle and horses without knowing something of the facts of life. It just happens that what you call desire is something very precious to me. I don't consider it something to be satisfied constantly as one would satisfy hunger. Maybe some time I'll meet a man that I can love—and respect. When I do I want to be in a position to demand his love and his respect in return."

"Sunday School stuff!" he scoffed. "I've known other girls like you, teasers. Let men hug 'em and kiss 'em and fondle 'em, but draw the line—"

"That isn't so!" She was rigid now and the hazel eyes were blazing. "Never since I was a child has a man kissed me on the lips but my father and my brother!"

He gave her a sour, knowing grin. "You sure of that?"

Memory of that first kiss from Bill reached her, and the blood slowly stained her cheeks. He saw the hint of tears on her lashes.

"That was—unfair!" she said brokenly. "You took me by surprise. I didn't realize what I was doing!"

"Like hell you didn't!"

"All right then, I did know! But for the moment I thought you might be that man—my man! Because you covered me and went away when you might—" She broke off, the flush deepening. "Every girl dreams of a Prince Charming, a knight without fear or reproach. I thought for a few silly seconds that my dream had come true. Then I knew how horribly wrong I was. And I tell you this, Bill Serviss, so that you'll know that never will I return your kiss. You're big and strong and ruthless; you can grab me whenever you're close enough to lay hands on me. I'm too weak to defend myself. You can hug me to you and kiss me and—and fondle me, but all the while I'll be thinking what a beastly coward you are to steal from me what you can't get honestly, and I'll hate you every day of my life."

She blinked and Bill saw tears on her cheeks. She turned away suddenly and sank into a chair and covered her face with her hands. She didn't sob, but he could see her shoulders shaking. It was a unique and disturbing position in which Bill found himself and for once he did not know what to do.

He cleared his throat and said, "Aw, now, Pat! Don't—don't cry like that. I thought—Aw, hell!" He turned and strode through the doorway.

His impotence angered him. He'd never got himself mixed up with such a—prude. And her father and brother probably cow thieves! By God, if he could pin the rustling on them he'd be able to tell her where to head in! He halted in the dismal back yard and gazed about him. He wanted to do something violent, something that would work off the anger. He saw a lean-to on the side of the cabin and strode to it. A rusty hasp was secured to a rusty staple by a wooden peg; he yanked this out and the door sagged on one leather hinge.

There was a miscellaneous assortment of junk in the lean-to and he prowled around examining it and tossing it aside. He didn't know what he was looking for until he came to a stack of tanned cowhides. He started peeling one off another in order to examine the brands.

He found several different brands, including some ET's, but the hides were all tanned and evidently old. Sam or Jim could have bought them and probably had; if they were from stolen stock even such a slipshod pair would not be so foolish as to keep the evidence of their guilt right here on their property. It would be interesting to hear what Pat had to say about them.

He started for the back door, slowed his steps, halted. Memory of Pat sitting there crying disturbed him. He turned with a muttered curse at his own weakness and got into his saddle. He sent the horse lunging through the sand and headed him in the direction of Pandora.

It was supper time when he reached town and he went directly to the restaurant. For some reason the tenderloin steak and hashed-browns failed to appeal and he had to force himself to eat. In a savage mood he made his camp by the spring and walked to the Silver Saddle.

Cleve Morley was there, and Bill asked him, "Do the Larkins have any other income besides what they pick up at odd jobs and prospecting?"

"No, I don't think so," answered Morley slowly. "Pat does some crocheting and—oh, yes! They buy up hides once in a while and tan them. Not many. Only market is the local cobbler and harness maker. Why?"

"Just wondering. Thanks."

Bill broke a rule of long standing and drank heavily that night. He was rugged and big and had the ability to conceal the outward effects of the alcohol. The passion in him helped to neutralize it; the picture of Pat with her hands over her face and the strands of dark hair peeping through her spread fingers was ever with him.

Gloria had ignored him and he hadn't noticed her; now, around midnight, she slipped up beside him at the bar, took his arm and smiled up into his face.

"Gonna buy a gal a drink, cowboy?" she asked coquettishly.

"You're damned right I am!" Bill called to a bartender. "Two double whiskeys and another one for a chaser."

They drank.

"How about a little roulette stake?" coaxed Gloria.

"I don't play parlor games," he said roughly. "Listen, wench; I'm camping down by the spring again tonight. Be around."

"Indeed!" Gloria became haughty. "And if I have other plans?"

"Cancel 'em, or I'll come back here and slap hell out of you."

He turned abruptly and strode away, and Gloria glared after him with anger in her blue eyes. Who did he think he was, ordering her around? He could take a good, long jump into the middle of nowhere!

Anger died and was replaced by surprise. Was it possible that she had Bill Serviss in the breadline at last? Where should she put him? She considered swiftly and found the answer almost at once. She hadn't liked the look on his face when he'd promised to slap hell out of her. He looked as though he'd enjoy keeping that promise and Gloria didn't relish having the hell slapped out of her. She also broke a rule of long standing and placed Bill right at the top.

Perhaps the memory of that one night they had spent together influenced her decision.

CHAPTER EIGHT

Cleve Morley stood at the bar and watched the interchange between Bill and Gloria with smug complacency. Gloria was his woman; he had her right under his thumb and Bill wouldn't get to first base with her. When Bill turned away and strode out of the place Cleve was sure that he had been given the brush-off. He felt warm and self-satisfied, like the owner of a one-man dog.

Thoughts of Gloria faded with Bill's exit and his mind went to another girl, a slim, shapely, dark-haired girl with hazel eyes. He thought often of Pat Larkin. He began thinking of her the very day she came into the basin and his desire for her had grown with the passage of the months until it had become an obsession. Some day he would have her.

Being a gentleman, his approach was indirect. He must play the game in accordance with well-established rules. The little tricks of courtesy came first; the swift doffing of the hat, the instant friendly smile, soft-voiced conversation, ready deference, those thousand little things that the gentleman does to convince his lady that he would never, by word or deed, place her on a plane lower than that occupied by a Heavenly Angel.

That wins her confidence and respect. After that it's a lot easier. Friendliness becomes casual intimacy; the gentleman turns brotherly or fatherly, depending on his age. An arm falls about a slim waist naturally and, to her, thoughtlessly. One can indulge in a little mild horseplay, pinch a pink cheek or a rounded arm. All in fun, of course. Then it's a case of waiting for the right time, the right place and the receptive mood.

That night outside the Larkin cabin, the time and the place were right, Morley had thought the mood right, too. Bill Serviss had just finished throwing his weight around; he had practically accused Pat's father and brother of being rustlers, had bullied Jimmy and treated Pat like a clod of dirt. She should have snatched at his offer to escape the whole sordid mess. But she hadn't.

Morley couldn't understand that. All women yearn for nice clothes, jewelry, servants to wait upon them. All the women that he had known would have given a lot more than their virtue to possess these things. And Pat had asked him (he had missed the irony) if he were proposing marriage! And he had been forced to stall. Maybe. Later on. For some reason it hadn't gone across. And now desire had become a live thing, eating at his vitals.

He stood scowling down at his untouched drink. If he could get some hold on her, a club to threaten or coerce. If for instance, he could uncover evidence that would convict her father and brother of rustling. Pat was a loyal soul and she loved her father and brother. Especially Jimmy; she was always willing to go to bat for Jimmy.

His recent conversation with Bill gave him an idea. Suppose that evidence was in the pile of hides at the Larkin cabin? It was conceivable that the ones who had rustled Thayer's steers might have found it necessary to destroy one of the animals because of injury. The remains would be buried, of course. Except in the case of one who was tanning and selling hides. Such a one might pack the hide along with him.

Morley stared a moment longer at his drink, then picked up the glass, swallowed the drink and thereafter felt quite cheerful. He made a round of the place, talking with the men he knew, watching the play and then moving on. Gloria had attached herself to a miner with a poke of dust and was seeing to it that he got rid of it in the most rapid and efficient manner. Her eyes were bright and her peach-bloom cheeks slightly flushed.

Cleve was smoking his third cigar of the evening when she came over to him. It was after midnight and the crowd was thinning. She said, "Darling, I have one of those horrible headaches. All right if I turn in?"

"Go right ahead," said Cleve amiably. "Sleep the clock around."

She raised perfectly arched eyebrows. "You kiddin'?"

"I'll even give you my key if you want it."

"I'll take your word for it, darling. Sleep tight—and alone."

"Same to you." He was feeling so good that he smiled at her.

She went out through the back door and he strolled after her and saw her turn into the covered stairway which led to the living quarters upstairs. In the act of returning to the saloon he changed his mind and went out into the cool night air. He closed the door behind him, took off his hat and for a few moments stood breathing deeply and enjoying the soft breeze.

A reluctance to re-enter the close, smelly saloon gripped him. He walked slowly across the alley and sat down on the edge of the watering trough outside the stable. There was no moon and his dark clothes made him a vague shadow against the deeper blackness. He tossed away the stub of the cigar, took off his hat and leaned back against the wooden pump. He thought again of Pat and closed his eyes.

If he dozed, it was for only a few minutes, and when his eyes snapped open he remained sitting there, quiet and watchful. His gaze was on the black oblong of the door which opened on the outside stairs. A crack of light from the bracket lamp in the hall above showed along its edge.

The crack widened, the black oblong became a sickly yellow and framed a human figure. It was that of Gloria, and she was wearing a long fur coat. He grinned sourly. Probably coming out for air.

She stepped into the alley and the oblong became black again. He hadn't heard the door close; she was being awfully quiet about it. She stood in the shadow of the building for a few moments, peering about her, then turned to her right and glided along the alley. When the shadows had swallowed her Cleve got up and followed, keeping close to the sheds and stables at the back of the alley.

He walked quietly and paused occasionally to listen. He did not hear her, and when he reached the end of the alley she was not in sight. He frowned and returned, this time walking along the back of sheds and stables, remembering the story she had told him that other night of resting with her back against a wall. When he failed to find her he went back to the alley and searched along the rear of the buildings on its other side.

His failure to locate her irked him. The dog, for once, had slunk away from the heel of its master. He returned by way of the street thinking that she might have seated herself on a dark doorstep. She hadn't.

His irritation became anger. What the hell was she doing roaming around town at one in the morning? Suspicion awoke. Had she sneaked out to meet someone? Bill Serviss? If she had he'd twist her neck! It wasn't jealousy which stirred him, it was injured ego.

He considered. Where would she meet Bill? In some deserted shack? No; Bill was an outdoors man. Where would he camp? He thought carefully. When Bill left that night he had turned to his left. What suitable camping site lay in that direction? The grove of trees just outside of town. There was a spring there and pasture for his horse.

Morley swung about and walked determinedly along the street.

He reached the last building and saw the dark mass which was the trees against the starlit sky. He walked over the uneven terrain, has boots making no sound on the soft earth and turf. At the edge of the trees he stopped to look and listen. There was no sound and he moved ahead stealthily, feeling the way with cautious feet. And then he saw the soft glow of light and knew he had located Bill's camp.

Bill looked first to his horse to make sure the animal had not fouled his picket line, then started a fire and unrolled his bed and spread it. The walk in the cool air had cleared his brain somewhat, but his head still buzzed and he felt foggy. He brewed and drank some coffee and felt better. Getting drunk was a damned fool thing to do on a job like this. Fellow never knew when somebody would take a potshot at him from the brush or spit in his face and dare him to draw. Damn Pat Larkin! She had driven him to it.

He knew that this was not so. No girl alive could *drive* him to do what he didn't want to do. It was realization that this case was getting him down that had forced him to seek artificial relaxation. Oh, sure he had Cole Brent and the Larkins and Pink Paradine and the other three as suspects, but that's all they were—suspects. He didn't have a blamed thing on any of them. And he had been on the job—how long? Aw, the devil with it!

He remembered a bit vaguely that he had ordered Gloria to report for night duty. That she would show up he did not in the least doubt. Gloria was fascinated by him. Treat them differently than other men do and they always are.

He pulled off his boots, stripped to his birthday suit and got between blankets. He lay there smoking and looking up through the trees at the stars. He wasn't in the mood to dally with Gloria, not while he was thinking of Pat, but he'd have to go through with it now.

She came stealing out of the gloom and into the firelight like a woodsprite, and he could see the avidness in her eyes by the light of the flames. "Right here, wench," he said.

She looked down at him, slowly unbuttoned the long coat. She kept it about her until the last moment, then with a shrug of her shoulders shook it from her. It fell at her feet and she stood, tall and slim, her warm flesh glowing in the soft light. She stepped over his long legs and dropped gracefully to her knees and bent over him. Her back was to the fire but even in the gloom her eyes were luminous.

"You damn' big he-brute!" she said between passion-tight lips. "You damn'—big—"

He reached up and seized her.

It was the harsh escape of pent-up breath as much as the crack of the stick which aroused Bill. He came swiftly to his knees, his hand reaching for the gun beside him. He froze, not attempting to snatch it up.

The fire had died down but there was still light, and by it he could see Cleve Morley and the derringer which was pointed at him. Morley's face was twisted with rage and his finger was taut on the trigger of the short double-barreled pistol.

Gloria had turned and was lying on her stomach, her blonde bead raised, her blue eyes, bright with fear, gazing at Morley. If ever she had seen murder in a man's face she was seeing it now.

Bill saw it too and reacted instantly. He let his muscles relax.

"Oh, it's you, Cleve. Thought at first one of those rustlers had caught me with my pants down. Why all the melodrama?"

The derringer shifted slightly so as to cover Gloria. Morley grated, "You lousy little slut!"

Bill pushed himself to his haunches. He said mildly, "I don't get it, Cleve. When I asked you the other night whether my pick of your girls included Gloria you said it did if I could make the grade. Well, I made it. What's the kick? You married to the gal or something?"

The gentleman in Morley asserted itself. He *had* given Bill permission to approach Gloria and it wasn't considered sporting to welch on an agreement if there was any danger of its being brought home to you. And in this case everybody who'd ever been inside the Silver Saddle knew that Gloria was one of his girls and supposedly available to anybody who had the price. And of course no gentleman could claim Gloria as his legitimate property. He lowered the derringer, but his hot gaze remained fixed on the girl.

"I'm not blaming you, Serviss. It's this little bitch. She knows better than to sleep with anybody else."

Bill reached for his pants. He drew them on while he talked. "Don't blame her, Cleve. I scared her into it. I told her if she didn't show up I'd beat her up. I was drunk and she thought I meant it. Can't really blame her for wanting to keep those lovely features."

The derringer dropped lower, Gloria said earnestly, "That's the truth, Cleve. Honest to God it is!"

Bill pulled on his boots and stood up. "Just a little misunderstanding, Cleve." He took two strides and picked up Gloria's coat. He tossed it to her. "Better run along, wench."

Cleve stood frowning and uncertain as she shrugged into the coat and stood up. Bill pulled on his shirt. He said, "Go on home. I want to talk with Cleve a minute."

She slipped away fearfully, her eyes on the scowling Cleve. He made as though to follow her but Bill said, "Come over here and squat, Cleve. I said I wanted to talk with you."

Cleve watched her disappear among the trees, then reluctantly came over to the fire. He didn't sit down. "What do you want?"

"Sit down and relax. You'd think she was the only woman in the world."

Morley let his breath out in a gust and dropped to the blanket.

Bill was rolling a cigarette. He said, "I'm sort of surprised at you, Cleve. You're a man of education and discernment; you can't tell me that you're all het up about this Gloria gal."

"It's not that. It's just that—well, I don't like people eating out of the same dish with me."

"I don't either; and when they do I get me another dish. Hell, a man of your attainments can aim higher than a dance-hall dolly. It's different when you raise 'em from pups, but this one's slept with a hundred men before you even set eyes on her." He lighted the cigarette, went on: "She's a satisfyin' wench, I'll grant you that; but a gentleman like you shouldn't feel compelled to go on the war-path over her."

"Maybe you're right," said Morley tightly. He was thinking of Pat now.

"Sure I'm right. And the worst thing that you could do would be to go back there and wring her neck. Don't let her see that it means so much to you. Just ignore her and she'll come yappin' after you like a little dog."

"That's the way you work it, eh?"

"Hell, no! I'm just a roughneck and I'd probably whale the devil out of her. But you can't afford to do that. If she shows up with her face all lopsided folks'll know you did it and they wouldn't think much of you for it."

Morley was silent, and Bill puffed steadily on his cigarette. Finally, Cleve said quietly, "You're right, Bill. I'll do as you say. I'll let her strictly alone and get me another dish."

He got to his feet and pushed the derringer into the holster under his left arm. He put out his hand. "Shake on it. And forget what happened here tonight."

Bill took the hand and wrung it with evident sincerity. "Sure. Be seein' you, Cleve."

He sat there smoking and watching as Morley walked stiffly through the trees. When Morley had gone he pitched the cigarette butt into the fire, pulled off his boots and slid under the blanket.

Bill was essentially a man of action, but he also knew something about diplomacy.

CHAPTER NINE

BILL WAS UP with the dawn and on his way by daybreak. He was still impatient at his failure to get ahead; he had tried waiting and he had tried stirring things up, and while there had been a few positive results he was still uncertain about Cole Brent, about the Larkins, and even about the Pandora marshal and the three who a-prospecting had gone.

There remained the two who had ambushed him that day and had chased him to the Larkin homestead. If he could identify either of them he might get a lead. He had tried to identify them in a casual manner. He had not had a good look at the one who had escaped; he knew the man was dark, with black stubble on his face, a bit on the heavy side. He rode a bay horse and wore levis and a work shirt of faded blue.

The one who had got his head in front of Bill's bullet was of medium build, with brown hair worn rather long, pale blue eyes and a sweeping moustache. He was one of a very common type of cowhand. Bill was riding his horse and had hoped that somebody would recognize the animal and inquire how it had come into his possession. The animal was neck-branded with a small JP which Bill assumed were the initials of its owner. But no one had questioned him about the horse and he hadn't met or heard of a man whose initials were JP. He had asked Morley about them when he had talked to Cleve right after leaving the Larkin homestead, and Morley had been unable to place them. He hadn't asked anybody else because there wasn't anybody else in whom he dared confide. For that matter, at this stage of the game, he was taking even what Morley told him with a few grains of salt.

No matter how impatient it made him he was back to watchful waiting again; waiting for the Larkins to show up, waiting for Paradine and Texas Tom and Swat and Harvey Short to return; waiting for Cole Brent to say or do something that would brand him a liar, waiting for the rustlers to try another steal.

At the moment the Larkins were the most important. They knew that Bill suspected them; if they returned it would be by stealth and their visit would probably last no longer than necessary to re-outfit. The others would hang around Pandora, for Bill had refrained from hinting even to Morley that they were suspects.

Bill rode to the hills back of the Larkin homestead, noticed that the one horse was still in the corral, then hung around until noon. Pat came out of the house several times. He studied her through the glasses and felt the hunger for her grow within him. He ate a scanty dinner and rode away, circling the basin and following the trail to Brent's ranch.

There was nobody about and once more he tramped through house and crew's quarters probing and prying. Nothing. He zigzagged around the basin, eyeing brands. Nothing but Candlestick stuff; Brent certainly kept his range well combed. He rode on to the trail which ran north and south and, just to make his investigation complete, turned north. There had been fresh prints leading in that direction but they were gone now, dust-covered and washed by rain.

He turned back after an hour or so. North was not the logical direction to drive stolen cattle. He pressed southward until, late in the afternoon, he was across the border. There was no marker to show where the boundary ran, but presently he came to a little Mexican town and went into a shabby cantina. He saw no other American and did not talk to any of the occupants but the proprietor. Bill's knowledge of Spanish was good and he spent the time listening. He heard no mention of cattle. The proprietor served him with dinner and furnished grain for his horse. When he had finished he rode around the little town, listening and watching. Nothing. He headed north once more.

It was dark when he passed the Candlestick and he could see light in the ranch house and in the crew's quarters. He did not stop, but pressed on until he reached the Larkin homestead. He pushed down into the basin and walked his horse soundlessly through the sand to a point a hundred yards from the house.

He tied his horse to a scrub oak and stole past the cabin to the corral. The house was dark and silent and he found just the one horse in the corral. He returned, stripped off his gear and picketed the horse, then unrolled his blankets, pulled off his boots, laid his hat and gunbelt where he could reach them easily and proceeded to sleep.

He awoke suddenly, habit keeping him perfectly quiet except for the flutter of eyelids. He lay there listening. In the deep silence he heard what sounded like the grate of metal against metal. It came from behind the house. He sat up, slipped the Colt from the holster and got to his feet. There was no time to draw on his boots; he stole silently on stockinged feet toward the shadow of the cabin, then moved along its side wall to the back.

He stood at the corner of the shack stabbing at the darkness with his eyes. He heard no sound, but movement ahead of him and to his left stiffened him. A dark blot glided across the range, indistinguishable except as a blur against the blackness of the hills beyond. Bill snapped up his gun then lowered it. The distance was too great and the light was poor. He started running, saw the shadow become part of a greater shadow, heard the soft thud of hoofs.

Bill halted. He couldn't hope to overtake a mounted man even if he had boots on. He turned back, went to the kitchen door and pounded on it. After a while he heard the soft shuffle of feet and Pat's voice said, "Who is it?"

"Bill Serviss. Let me in."

"No. Go away."

"Listen, sister; you open that door or I'll break it down. I want to give this shack a good going over."

The tight voice said, "Wait a minute."

Footsteps receded, then returned. He heard the bar being removed and the door swung open. Pat was standing with a lamp in one hand; the other clutched a blanket which she had drawn about her. The dusky hair hung over her shoulders and the hazel eyes were fear-stricken.

"What do—" She stopped, remembering the other time she had asked him what he wanted. "Why are you here?"

He answered gruffly. "I told you. To search the cabin. Your father and brother were here, weren't they?"

"No. I haven't seen them since the evening they left."

"In a pig's eye you haven't. Somebody just left here. I saw him."

She shook her head, a little frown wrinkling her brow. "Nobody has been inside the cabin. That's the truth."

He glared at her fiercely but her eyes did not falter, and finally he let his gaze search the kitchen. It was neat and orderly; there were no signs of dirty dishes or odors of cooked food. And if the Larkins had come home they would surely have eaten.

He walked about, peering behind the stove, looking into cupboards. He said, "Give me thc lamp," and when she did so carried it into the other room. Here, too, everything was in order. The bunks were neatly made up, each chair was in its place. He went about the room examining everything. He pulled aside the curtain which divided the room and saw her bed with its covers thrown back just as she had left it. He put his hand on the sheet and found it warm from her body. He hesitated, then pushed his hand under the covers and felt beside the spot where she had lain. The sheet was cool to his touch.

He turned to find her watching him, scorn in her eyes. "There was no one sleeping with me," she said.

He felt his cheeks go warm. "I didn't think there was. But somebody was here at the cabin. Maybe not inside it, but here. And what would he want outside the place?"

"I don't know. It couldn't have been father or Jimmy or he would have come in. How did you know?"

"I was camped close by. Some sound woke me up. I sneaked up to the corner of the shack and saw somebody get on a horse and ride away."

"I haven't any idea who it was. I was asleep and the doors were barred and the windows locked. Although," the scorn was back in her voice, "my right to privacy doesn't seem to mean a thing to you."

Again he felt his cheeks go warm and the knowledge that she could put him on the defensive angered him. "No, your privacy doesn't mean a thing to me. Why should it? I've already seen as much of you as there is to see. I'm doing a job of work and while I'm doing it I'll walk into any damn' place I want to at any time of the day or night if I think there's a chance of nailing the thieves on this range. And as long as Sam and Jim Larkin lie to me and play hide-and-seek I'm going to assume that they're the ones I'm after."

She drew back a pace, her eyes widening. "Lie?"

"Lie! That map your father gave me took me to a claim they'd worked all right, but not within a month. If Sam Larkin had nothing to hide, why did he pull a trick like that?"

There was distress in her eyes now and her face had gone white.

"I don't know. I don't. But there must be some reason. I'm sure of it. Dad and Jimmy would never steal."

"You'd be surprised at the people who'd steal if they thought they could get away with it. Here's your lamp; go back to bed. And wrangle me some breakfast in the morning; I'll be camped right outside."

He put the lamp into her hand and strode out leaving her clutching the blanket tightly about her. She followed him to the door and when he had closed it he heard the bar drop into place.

He stood there for a moment thinking. If the unknown visitor had not been inside the shack, what had he wanted? Bill walked over to the lean-to and pulled the peg from the staple; when he opened the door the hasp scraped along the staple making just such a sound as he had heard. He left the door sagging on its one hinge and went inside. He found a piece of paper and lighted it, using it as a torch. Nothing of interest here except the pile of hides and he had already examined them thoroughly.

He gave the place a final careful scrutiny before the light died, then shook his head impatiently and went out. He closed the door and got that scrape of hasp on staple again. Whoever had been here had opened that door. It was possible that Sam or Jim Larkin had spotted him when he rode down into the basin and had hidden there until they thought it safe to leave.

He went back to bed and slept until daylight. When he led the horse to the tank to water him, he saw smoke coming from the chimney of the shack. He picketed the animal, washed up at the bench outside the kitchen door, rapped and went inside. There was fire in the stove and Pat was beating up flapjack batter. The coffee pot was steaming and bacon sizzled. He said, "Good morning, Miss Larkin."

Her voice was coolly polite. "Good morning, Mr. Serviss."

"I really didn't expect you to get my breakfast."

"Why not? It's customary, isn't it? to feed anybody who comes to your home hungry. Even if he is your worst enemy."

"Yeah, it is." Bill was comfortable. He sat down and held his hat on his knees.

She worked deftly, quietly, apparently unaware of his steady regard. She set the table for one while the griddle heated, then poured out batter and pushed the coffee pot back. Presently she said, "Better eat them as I make them. They're better that way."

He put his hat on the floor, drew up a chair and started eating. She poured his coffee and served him in silence. When he had finished he got up and said, "It's your turn now."

"I'm not hungry. Really I'm not."

"Sit down."

Her chin came up and she eyed him defiantly for a moment; then she lowered her gaze and slipped into the chair.

He got plate and cup and saucer from the cupboard and knife, fork and spoon from a drawer and set them before her. He poured the batter and when it had baked on one side turned it by flipping it into the air and catching it on the griddle. He saw by the quick lighting of the hazel eyes that the trick interested and amused her. She ate two flapjacks but balked at the third. "Really, Bill, I can't eat another bite."

She had used his first name and he experienced a thrill of pleasure.

He smiled down at her. "You're sure?"

"Sure. They were delicious. Honest!"

For an instant there was warmth in the eyes that looked up at him, then the wariness crept back into them and she was on guard again. He said, "I'll help you with the dishes."

"No. That's the woman's job."

"It's customary for the hungry one to do something for his meal."

"I'd rather you wouldn't."

He did not press the point. "Okay, Pat. Thanks."

He picked up his hat and went out. He strode over to the woodpile, took up the rusted bucksaw and went to work. When he had cut and split a pile of wood he carried it into the kitchen and dumped it into the wood box. She said, "Thanks, Bill," and he said, "You're welcome," and went out. He was mildly amazed at his subdued behavior. So, incidentally, was she.

He spent the day loafing about in the hills surrounding the basin, keeping the place under observation. He was glad now that he had not fired at the intruder; perhaps he would return tonight.

He didn't. Bill camped near the cabin and slept with the mental alarm set. He awoke at dawn and stole away quietly, longing for another hot breakfast but unwilling to force Pat to the kindness. He camped in the hills and cooked his breakfast there. He continued to watch. He ate dinner in the same place and settled himself for some more waiting.

Toward the middle of the afternoon he spotted a rider crossing the basin from the direction of Pandora, and through his glasses recognized Cleve Morley. Cleve, he knew, visited the homestead frequently but today his visit held a new significance. Cleve was making a play for Pat and had told him the other night that he was going to find himself another dish.

Bill started for his horse, stopped and returned to his watching post. Why should he be worried about Cleve's visit. He sat down on a rock and watched as Morley rode to the rear of the cabin, tied his horse to a ring in the log wall, opened the door and walked in. Closed the door behind him.

Minutes passed. Long minutes. Bill got up and paced about, drawing strongly on his cigarette. He saw them come out, go to the lean-to, and enter it together, They left the door open but the gloom within was too deep for him to see what they were doing even through the glasses. Presently they came out and walked to the cabin. Cleve was holding Pat's arm and his form hid her from Bill's view. They went into the house and Bill did some more waiting.

He waited five minutes, then could endure it no longer. He strode to his horse, tightened the cinches, mounted and rode down into the basin. He rode swiftly at first, then slowed to a walk when he hit the stretch of sand.

And suddenly he heard Pat's voice. It was raised and the timbre of despair was in it. *"No! No!"* And then, shrill and sharp and hysterical, *"Bill!"*

He sank the spurs deep and the startled horse bounded forward.

CHAPTER TEN

As Cleve Morley had ridden toward the Larkin homestead his face was tight and determined, like that of a man who has nerved himself to a task which requires courage to undertake. His eyes were bright and there was sweat on his forehead. He rode stiffly in his saddle.

Glora had been still in her room sleeping when he'd left. She could sleep forever for all he cared. He had her guessing, he knew. He hadn't upbraided her or reproached her or, in fact, said one word to her since he had surprised her with Bill Serviss. He had simply ignored her and he knew she was puzzled and disturbed. She would have preferred a good cussing out and a poke in the puss; a grand free-for-all that would have ended up the usual way and all would have been well. But now Gloria did not know where she stood and she was worried and uncertain. Serviss was right; this was the way to treat them. He'd find himself another dish.

Morley rode slowly; he didn't want to get himself all hot and bothered and smelled up with horse sweat. He had washed and shaved and anointed himself with oil, and he chewed a clove to kill the whiskey odor acquired in the process of building up his courage. He felt himself quite irresistible.

It was mid-afternoon when he dismounted in the rear of the Larkin cabin. In the act of knocking he changed his mind, opened the door and walked boldly in. The kitchen was empty and he called, "Anybody home?"

Pat answered from the inner room and he strode through the doorway. He hoped to find her in the act of changing her dress; the sight of her would fan the fire that blazed within him. Instead, he found her seated on the couch crocheting. She had been so absorbed that she had not seen him pass by the window and the sand had smothered the sound of hoofs.

He affected a bluff heartiness. "Hello, honey. Busy as ever, eh?"

He went over and sat down beside her and she lowered the crocheting to her lap. "Busy as ever," she repeated mechanically.

He bent over to examine the work. "Fancy stuff, isn't it? Don't see how you do it. Don't even see *why* you do it. You should be buying stuff like that instead of selling it." He glanced up quickly. "Thought over my proposition?"

"I told you there was nothing to think over, Cleve."

"And I told you there was. A nice, cozy home, just large enough for two. A cook and housekeeper and a maid. They'd sleep out, of course. A full pocketbook and charge accounts at the best stores. I'd say there was plenty to think over, honey."

She sighed. "It's no use, Cleve. Maybe I'm silly, but the price seems a bit too high."

"Does it?" He stared at her for a moment in silence, then went on. "How about your father and Jimmy? I could do things for them. I could do a lot for them. I might even save them from—hanging."

She started and her features tightened. "What do you mean, Cleve?"

He shrugged. "Don't pretend, darling. Surely you must have some suspicion. What takes them away from home for such long stretches? Prospecting? Horse hunting? What have they to show for their prospecting and hunting?"

"They've found gold," she said angrily. "They've sold horses."

"How much gold? How many horses? To keep you living in a dump like this! Wake up, honey. Where were they the night Thayer's cattle were stolen?"

She stared at him with fright in her eyes. She didn't know.

He went on casually. "I know they're stealing stock. Bill Serviss is sure they're rustling. He went into the hills to hunt for them and is probably on their trail right now. And I'd stake my life that I could find evidence of their guilt right here on the homestead if I were to look for it."

"You could not. Bill Serviss searched the place just the other day."

"Did he search the lean-to?"

"Well—no. But there's nothing out there but junk."

"Want to bet?"

"Yes!"

He got up. "Let's go and see."

She followed him readily enough. They went out through the kitchen and Morley pulled the peg from the staple and yanked open the door. They went inside. It was gloomy, but there was light enough to see. She indicated the junk with a disdainful gesture. "Do you see any evidence?"

He looked about him thoughtfully, his gaze passing over the disordered articles which littered the place. He said, "Are you sure Sam and Jimmy bought all those hides?"

"Of course I am!"

He walked over to the pile, looked down at it a moment, then started moving the hides, making another pile. They were hard and stiff. He moved half a dozen of them, then she heard his gasp of triumph. She asked quickly, "What is it?"

He pointed to the hide he had just uncovered. "Feel it."

Pat touched the hide, felt its softness. It was new and it had not yet been tanned. She bent over and saw the ET brand on it. She said, "Oh, no!"

Morley said nothing. He repiled the hides, hiding the new one. Pat watched him, the disbelief in her eyes changing slowly to doubt. She said again, faintly, "Oh, no!"

Morley finished, looked about him, said, "Come on in." She followed him outside, dazed and pitiful. He closed the door and replaced the wooden peg. He took her arm led her into the cabin, and she went ahead of him into the living room and sank down upon the couch. She shook her head as one trying to rid himself of some awful memory.

Morley said softly, "See what I mean?"

She looked at him, a desperate appeal in her eyes. "Cleve, you won't tell on them. You can't!"

"I can. I should. Whether or not I do depends on you."

She knew what he meant and shook her head. "No, Cleve. Please! You're their friend, my friend. Let me talk with them; they'll listen to me. It'll never happen again. I promise you, Cleve. And we'll be grateful to you all our lives!"

"I don't want gratitude." The moment had come and Cleve's blood was pounding through his veins. "I want you Pat. I always have. Do what I ask and go away with me."

She put her face in her hands and rocked back and forth. "No, no, no, Cleve! It's wicked—it's wrong. I just can't!"

He dropped to the couch beside her; he put his arms about her and held her tightly. The contact of her body against his turned his blood to liquid fire. His hat fell to the floor and he put his lips close to her cheek.

"You can! Nobody'd know. You could tell your father and brother that we'd eloped. Even if they guessed the truth they couldn't do anything. Not after what we've found out about them today."

She broke away from him and turned a face that was blazing with anger.

"What must you think of me to suggest such a thing as that! To live with you—accept your money—lying to them, or even worse telling them the truth! Cleve Morley's mistress! A paid woman, like one of his dance-hall girls! No, I tell you, *no!*"

Cleve's face turned ugly. "That's final, is it?"

"Absolutely! I don't want ever to see you again! I'll ride up into the hills and find father and Jimmy myself and we'll go away from here. So far that Bill Serviss or nobody else will ever find us!"

"Then," said Morley thickly, "I'll give you a memory to take along with you!"

He reached out and grabbed her roughly.

She fought him, her young body like so much live steel. She got to her feet, dragging him with her; she twisted and turned like an eel to escape his greedy clutch; she struck at him and bit his hand. And he just suffered the blows and the bites and grinned at her with lust shining in his eyes.

Fight as she would, she could not get away from the fingers that had clamped on her arms like iron grapnels, They wrestled about the room, upsetting the table with the lamp on it, crashing into chairs. There was nothing of the gentleman remaining in Morley now; he was the caveman fighting to drag the female of his choice to his cave. And at last his superior strength told and her muscles tired and her resistance weakened and he pulled her slowly to him and got his arms about her and raised her from the floor.

It was then that she had cried, "No, no!" And then, simply because she knew that nobody could possibly be within reach of her voice but Bill Serviss, had cried with all her strength, *"Bill!"*

"Bill, eh?" panted Morley. "So that's how it is! Eating out of my dish again!"

He had reached the couch now, and with a last desperate rally of her failing strength Pat fought him anew. It was not a long fight; she was too exhausted. He stumbled over a throw rug and she fell on the couch, with him sprawled across her body. Her head was swimming and widening circles of blazing light were whirling before her.

And then came the rapid thud of boots across the kitchen floor and Morley jerked erect. He was on his knees by the couch and his eyes were fixed on the doorway like those of a waiting cougar.

Bill came into the room.

Just for an instant he hesitated, actually appalled by what he saw; but that instant was sufficient for Morley to spring to his feet and tear the derringer from the armpit holster.

He got it clear and that was all. A fist struck his arm so hard that the blow nearly broke his wrist and the gun went spinning into the air and fell on the floor. Then Bill was boring in and to Pat, watching from the couch, he was like some fearful avenging angel in his wrath.

He struck just two blows with his fist; the one that knocked the gun from Morley's hand and another that crashed against his mouth, loosening the teeth and splitting his lips. Then he worked with open palms, slapping the white cheeks with sounds like boards on water, hard, vicious swipes that bruised and punished.

Morley tried to fight back but he didn't stand a chance against this six-feet-two of brute strength and rage. He backed away, trying to avoid the blows, panting, half crying in his helplessness and pain. And at last he stumbled to his knees and rolled over on his face, a broken, beaten man.

Bill kicked him in the side, and it wasn't a gentle kick. "Get up, you slimy snake, and get the hell out of here before I kill you!"

Morley, groaning in agony, pushed himself to hands and knees and skittered like a drunken crab through the doorway and into the kitchen. He was headed for the back door when he heard Bill's voice in the other room.

"Pat, did that skunk harm you?"

The answer came weakly. "No. No, Bill."

Morley pulled himself to his feet and staggered through the doorway. With shaking fingers he untied the slip-knot in his rein and managed, by standing on the step, to pull himself into the saddle. Then, mounted and ready for flight, rage and spite and the desire for vengeance gripped him. He called back through the open doorway. "You little bitch! You spawn of a thief! Show him that hide in the lean-to! And if he doesn't have that lousy father and brother of yours hanged, I'll have him run out of the country and do it myself!"

He had one glimpse of the angry Bill coming into the kitchen and spurred desperately around the corner of the cabin. He rode hard, bent low in the saddle, until he was out of rifle range. Then he looked back fearfully, expecting to find Bill in pursuit. But there was no one in sight and he sat erect with a sigh of relief.

He rode a bit farther, slowed to a walk, looked back again. He halted the horse and turned him. He took out a handkerchief and dabbed at his bloody mouth, cursing when he felt the loose, aching teeth. The fear within him diminished with realization that he was out of Bill's reach, and rage caught fire and burned.

Who the hell did Serviss think he was, playing knight errant? The bastard had slept with Gloria and Maybelle and God alone knew how many more. There could be but one reason for his rage; he was in love with Pat and had probably slept with her, too.

He waited long minutes, several times wheeling the horse but always reining him around again. What was keeping the bastard? Probably collecting his reward. Mixed with his anger was injured ego. Damned if any man would eat out of his dish without paying for it! But he must see for himself.

He started back towards the cabin, riding slowly, ready to turn and flee at first sight of Bill. He angled to his left so as to approach the shack on its blind side. He reached a corner of the building, halted to listen, then inched the horse to the edge of a window, leaned from the saddle and peered into the room.

Bill was standing on the far side of the room. He stood stiffly, with his hands clenched at his sides and he was staring across the room with eyes that burned. Cleve turned his head to follow the direction of his gaze.

Pat had come out of the room which had been partitioned off for herself. She, too, stood stiffly with hands clenched. Her head was held high and the whiteness of her face contrasted with the dusky hair which fell about her shoulders. Her arms and throat were bare and she was wearing nothing but the sheerest of night-gowns, the creases of newness still in it.

He saw Bill extend his arms and start forward, desire flaming in his eyes. This was too much for Cleve. With a muttered oath of rage he reined his horse about and sent it lunging with a vicious jab of spurs.

CHAPTER ELEVEN

BILL HAD STOOD in the middle of the disordered room after Morley had gone, looking down at the girl on the couch. She lay limp and exhausted, her hair disheveled, her face startlingly white. He said, "Pat, did that skunk harm you?" and she shook her head and said, "No. No, Bill." She turned her face to the wall and started to cry. She was trembling.

Morley's voice reached them through the outside doorway. "You little bitch! You spawn of a thief! Show him that hide in the lean-to! And if he doesn't have that lousy father and brother of yours hanged, I'll have him run out of the country and do it myself!"

Bill started for him at a run, turned into the kitchen just in time to see Morley's distorted face vanish. He ran as far as the corner of the cabin and watched the coward fleeing as though the devil were after him. Bill shrugged and turned back. He could overtake Morley, perhaps, but he had already beaten him to his knees and further punishment would bring only unconsciousness. He could kill him, but what could he gain? Morley hadn't harmed Pat; Bill wouldn't have even the excuse of rape to back him.

The hide in the lean-to. What hide? Bill had examined the pile and had found nothing wrong. But somebody had visited that lean-to since his examination. If that somebody was Sam or Jim Larkin, he might have returned to secrete a new hide in the pile. If there was a new hide.

He turned to the lean-to, pulled the peg and opened the sagging door. He glanced about, saw no loose hide, then started working on the pile. He found it almost at once, felt its softness, judged its age and had his suspicions of the Larkins confirmed. The chance of its having been bought was about one in a thousand.

He rolled the hide and tied it to his saddle. Morley would testify that it had been in the lean-to, and perhaps Thayer could identify it by its markings as coming from one of his rustled steers. At least Thayer could tell him whether it had been bought from him.

He went into the shack to find Pat sitting up on the couch. Her face was still white but she had regained her composure and some of her strength. Her eyes questioned him and he said, "It was there, all right. Morley was holding it over you, wasn't he?"

She nodded dumbly. The picture was quite clear in his mind.

"He wanted you and thought he could get you by promising to forget it, and when you turned him down he tried to take you by force."

She said in a dry voice, "What are you going to do?"

"Bring them in if I can find them. There isn't anything else I can do."

Animation returned to her. Her face came alive, but she spoke slowly.

"You could give them a chance to get out of the country. You could say you couldn't find them."

He shook his head, his eyes cold. "When I took this job I swore to uphold the law without fear or favor. I don't take my oaths lightly. Rustling is one of the rottenest crimes in the West; what kind of a man would you think me if I deliberately let them go?"

"The kind of man that I'd do anything for!"

He raised an eyebrow cynically. "Anything?"

"Anything!" She was sitting erect and stiff on the couch, her hazel eyes holding his. She saw the hunger for her in his face.

He took a step forward, halted, forced himself to speak calmly. "God knows I want you, Pat. I want you so much it hurts. I think of you all day and dream of you at night. I see you as you were when I put you down on the bed—and walked out. I'm human, but you can't buy me. And I'm not Cleve Morley to use my knowledge to force something from you that you wouldn't give of your own free will."

She got up slowly and stood facing him, her chin high. Her voice broke as she spoke. "If you save them for me, Bill, I—I'll give you what you want. Of my own—free will."

"You're lying!" he accused harshly.

"I'm not!" Her muscles went lax; she took a step towards him, stopped, stood twisting her hands together, shaking her head from side to side. She spoke rapidly, pleadingly. "You've got to let them go! They don't know that hide was found; they'll be coming in for supplies any day now unless they're warned. Find them, Bill, and tell them to get out of the country! Cleve will talk about that hide and everybody will be looking for them. Find them and warn them!"

His jaws were tight. "You're talking crazy talk. I've got to bring them in now or Morley'll swear I deliberately let them go, and he'd be right. I've got to fetch them back even if they're on the other side of the border."

She stood looking at him helplessly, all the desperate entreaty that she could summon in her face. She was leaning forward slightly, her arms extended beseechingly. He turned his back to her and strode to a window.

She dropped her arms, slowly straightened. The entreating look left her face and was replaced by one of desperate resolve. She whispered, "Wait a minute." When he finally turned the curtained entrance to her room still stirred.

He waited, puzzled. What trick was she up to now? Probably gone to get her rifle. Well, she could shoot him if she wanted to; he was not for sale. He waited, heard the rasp of a bureau drawer. He glanced about, saw the Winchester standing in the corner. It wasn't the rifle she had gone for; probably a revolver. The curtains parted and he stepped back a pace, gasping in sheer surprise.

Pat came into the room slowly. She held her head high and her face was no longer white but stained with the pink of embarrassment and shame. She had let her dark hair down over her shoulders and she moved stiffly like a sleepwalker. Her hands were clenched nervously at her sides. She was wearing a sheer nightgown and against the light from the window he could see her softly curved figure.

He took an involuntary step forward, his arms extended, then he stopped abruptly and for a moment they both stood and stared at each other. Ten men could have been gazing at them through the window and they would not have known. She had tried to force what she imagined to be a seductive look into her eyes, but he read there only fear and utter shame. Her gaze faltered, her lids fluttered down, the dark head drooped. "I—I'm ready. Take me, Bill."

He leaped forward, seized her and drew her close. He kissed her hair, her eyes, her throat. He found her lips and they clung to his. And then he felt moisture on his cheek and through the red haze saw the tears which sparkled on her lashes.

"No! By God, no!"

He thrust her roughly from him, stood regarding her, panting. She sank to her knees on the floor before him. "Please, Bill!" she begged. "Please!"

He lashed out at her, struck her on the side of the head with the palm of his hand. She toppled over and lay there, sobbing, the dark hair falling about her. He spoke rapidly, angrily, releasing his passion in words, using those words to discipline himself.

"I told you I'm no Cleve Morley! You know damned well that you're lying to me with every breath in your beautiful body. You've offered yourself like a streetwalker to save that worthless father and brother of yours. I'm not in the market! I'm not buying! Keep your damned virtue until you're ready to give it to me, not using it to get what isn't mine to give!"

He strode out of the room, moving fast. He didn't look back and he didn't pause. He snatched up the rein of his waiting horse and vaulted into the saddle in the same movement; he wheeled the animal with a savage jerk and drove the spurs deep. He pushed the laboring horse through the sand at a full gallop, let him run full out for over a mile before he checked the pace.

The wind tearing at his face took some of the fire with it; he shook his head to clear his brain and relaxed his taut muscles. He breathed deeply and looked about him. Nearing the far side of the basin was a horseman and he knew it to be Cleve Morley. He was in no state of mind to wonder why the fellow had got no farther since leaving the cabin. He had no idea how much time had elapsed.

The vision of Pat remained and he berated himself viciously. Once more the gates of Paradise had been opened to him and once more he had walked away from them. What in hell was wrong with him? What were the lives of two lousy cow thieves compared with that which had been offered him? When had he become so goddam holy about this rotten job? Why hadn't he taken her up, found the Larkins, sent them across the border, then returned to claim his reward? After the first time there would be no end until he willed it. And he had turned her down! She had knelt before him and begged him to take her and he had turned her down! Good suffering Judas, what a fool!

He was within sight of Pandora before he had himself fully under control. He realized he'd have to watch his step now. He had made a mortal enemy of Cleve Morley and Morley was a power in the community. Morley also belonged to the Cattlemen's

Association and had been one of those who had hired Bill. Morley had seen the hide in the lean-to and would expect Bill to act promptly on the evidence. Well, there was just one check Bill must make before he did so. He turned away from Pandora and set out for Thayer's ranch.

Dusk was falling when he rode into the ET yard and he knew by the smoke which came from the chimney that Thayer's supper was being prepared. Ed himself came out on the gallery. He said, "You're just in time for supper, Serviss. Light your saddle and come in."

Bill stepped down, declined the invitation. "No, thanks; I can't stay. I got something to show you and then I'll be on my way." He unstrapped the hide and spread it and Thayer came down from the gallery to look at it.

"Where'd you get that?" Thayer looked up and his voice was sharp.

"Tell you in a minute. You recognize it?"

"Hell, yes! It came off'n one of those rustled steers. All my boys know those markin's because the steer was lame and we were doctorin' it."

"You didn't destroy that steer and sell the hide?"

"No, by God!"

"You're sure that none of your men did without your knowing it?"

"Certain! Serviss, where did you get that hide?"

"From a pile in Sam Larkin's lean-to. It was the only new one and the only one that wasn't tanned."

"Then they're the ones we want!"

"They're the ones you're going to get."

"By Judas, boy, you fetch them in and I'll pay you a bonus outa my own pocket! But come in and eat before you start."

"Can't, thanks. I've got to go to Pandora. Cleve Morley saw the hide in the lean-to and I want to make sure that he'll testify to it."

He tied the hide back on the saddle and set out for Pandora. It was around eight o'clock when he got there and when he entered the Silver Saddle Morley was not in sight. He asked a bartender where Cleve was.

"Up in his room, I reckon. He ain't come down yet."

Bill went outside, got the hide, tucked it under his arm and went around back to the covered stairway. He climbed the stairs quickly, stopped in the hall and looked about him. Morley would have the best room, of course. That would be the front one.

Bill had the hide under his left arm. He walked to the door of the front room, tried the knob and found it unlocked. He heard Cleve ask, "What is it?" and pushed the door open and stepped inside. His right hand had moved from knob to revolver butt but Morley clearly had not expected a visit from him, for he was lying on the bed, a cold towel on his face. His eyes blazed when he recognized Bill and he jerked up on the bed.

"Goddam you! You got your nerve, coming here!"

"I didn't come to ask about your health." Bill unrolled the hide and spread it on the floor, then turned up the lamp which stood on a dresser. "Is this the hide you spotted in the Larkin lean-to?"

Morley glanced at it. "Yes."

"I just showed it to Ed Thayer. He says it came from one of his stolen steers. I'm going after the Larkins and when I fetch them in I want you to testify that you saw the hide in their lean-to."

"I'll testify. You just see that you fetch them in."

Bill was folding the hide. "I'll fetch them in."

"If that little—" Morley remembered in time and changed it. "If the girl gets word to them, they'll light out over the border."

"I can cross the border, too."

"You can't arrest them on that side."

"I can drag 'em back and arrest 'em on this side. I got no respect for the rights of rustlers."

He went out and closed the door. From the alley he walked to the street, turned left and went down to the combination jail and marshal's office. There was a light inside and when he entered he expected to see Pink Paradine's night deputy. Instead he saw Paradine himself seated with his feet on a drawn desk drawer. Paradine said, "Hello, Serviss; what's on your mind?"

Bill put the hide on the desk. "I want you to take care of this for me. It's evidence, so don't let it get away from you. And give me a receipt for it."

Paradine opened the hide, examined it and whistled when he saw the brand. He asked Bill where he got it and Bill told him. Paradine grinned. "Looks like you got the goods on 'em, all right."

He wrote out a receipt and Bill pocketed it and went out. He had intended riding directly to the Larkin homestead to watch for Sam and Jim's appearance, but now that Paradine was back he stopped at the Silver Saddle in an effort to learn whether the prospectors had returned also.

Cleve Morley had come downstairs and was leaning against the bar in his accustomed place, trying to smoke a cigar and look nonchalant. *Probably told them he walked into a door,* thought Bill. He walked to the bar and ordered a drink, paying no attention to Morley. He studied the occupants of the room in the expensive back-bar mirror, but there were few customers and Texas Tom was not among them. He didn't know Swat Harrington and Harvey Short, so he was unable to determine whether the prospectors had returned with Pink Paradine.

A bartender was wiping the mahogany in front of Bill. He wiped industriously and was looking furtively in Morley's direction. Bill observed Cleve in the mirror, saw him turn his back to the bar and gaze towards the rear of the room.

The man said in a whisper through motionless lips. "Put your hand on the bar."

Bill let his left hand hand drop casually to the bar; the rag brushed his fingers and he felt the touch of paper. He closed his hand over it and the bartender moved away. Bill tossed off his drink, wiped his mouth, thrust the hand with the note into his chaps pocket and turned away. He loitered a moment at the faro table, then moved casually to the door and went outside. He walked along the street, stepped into a passageway between two buildings, peered about him, then thumbed a match into flame. The note read:

Bill, I must see you at once. Very important. Wait behind the stable; when the one who gives you this gives me the word I'll meet you there.

It was signed with a capital M. M stood for Maybelle; also it stood for Morley.

Bill grinned tightly and started for the alley.

CHAPTER TWELVE

Bill did not go directly to the back of the stable. Morley hated his guts, for Bill had not only thrashed him but also, far worse, had humiliated him before Pat Larkin. That was the unforgivable sin. Morley was quite capable of sending the note purporting to have come from Maybelle and then blasting Bill out of this world when he kept the appointment.

He emerged in the alley a hundred yards or so from the Silver Saddle, stood for a short while peering about him, then crossed and went out on the open range. He cut an arc which brought him almost a quarter of a mile in the rear of the saloon stable and then started working his way towards it. He walked in a crouch and finallly got to his hands and knees, his .44 Colt ready in his hand.

There was a faint moon and by its light he saw nothing to disturb him; but long before he reached the spot where he had decided to wait he caught sight of a blur of white behind the stable and identified it as the light-colored dress of a woman. From his position near the ground he called softly, "Maybelle!"

The figure advanced a short distance, then stopped. He said, "This way," and it came on again, faster now. He did not show himself, but directed the person by voice until he could recognize her; then he squatted on his heels and said, "Right here, cow gal. And get down low."

She crouched beside him, put a hand on his arm to steady herself. She spoke quickly, without preliminary. "Bill, they're back. Texas and Swat and Harvey Short."

"Also Pink Pardine. I was talking to him."

"They're a bad bunch, gunfighters, all of them, and they work together. I had to see you and tell you, for there's somethin' up. I know it. You had a fight with Cleve, didn't you."

"It wasn't a fight. I slapped hell out of him. I reckon I'd do it again under the same circumstances."

"He came in just before supper. I was in my room. It's next to Gloria's and he went in to see her. I tried to hear what they were saying but I couldn't. He was awful mad. When he came out I opened my door a crack and saw him. His mouth was swollen and cut and Gloria fetched a wet towel to him. He took it to his room with him and he didn't go out to supper. He's in the saloon now trying to act calm and collected but he's mad clean through. He said he walked into a post out in the stable and cut his lip on a nail. Bill, what happened?"

"He found a new hide in the Larkin lean-to. It had an ET brand on it. He tried to make a deal with Pat Larkin by which she could save her father and brother from arrest as rustlers and when Pat turned him down he tried to take what he wanted by force. I happened in on him."

"Why, the dirty so-and-so!" said Maybelle hotly. "I wish you'd killed him!"

He observed her curiously. "Excuse my bad manners, but that sounds queer coming from you."

"I don't care how it sounds, Pat Larkin's a decent kid." She laughed shortly, bitterly. "Believe it or not, there are some decent women. Nearly all women are decent at heart; it's usually some low-down skunk of a man that makes 'em otherwise. Or sometimes somethin' happens to break them. Somebody they love dies and they just don't give a damn any more. Men get drunk to forget; they——"

She broke off and Bill felt the hand on his arm tremble. "If Joe had lived I'd 'a' been like Pat Larkin. I would 'a' made him a good wife and would 'a' had babies for him, and——" The hand was removed and he knew she was crying.

A wave of tenderness gripped him. He put his arms about her and drew her close to him. "Sure, kid, sure. I know. You *are* decent, and you'll make some man a good wife yet." Something seemed to be choking him.

"Oh, Bill!" She was on her knees now and clinging to him like a child to its father. "I'm so damned rotten! But I wouldn't have been! Honest I wouldn't! I kept thinkin' of Joe and of how happy we'd 'a' been, and everything was so d-damned gray and l-lonesome without him, and I—I——"

"Sure, sure." His voice was husky. "Hush up now, cow gal. Get that chin in the air. You've got a lot of life ahead of you and there's a lot of good men left in this old world."

She pushed herself gently away and dabbed at her eyes. She did not speak for a full minute and when she did her voice was composed.

"No, Bill, there'll never be another. I'm bound to hell on a toboggan and the sooner the trip's over the better it'll be. But I ain't lyin' when I say there are good women and that Pat is one of them. You can tell it by the way she looks at you. Her eyes are honest. Not like mine, not like Gloria's. There's one woman that's really bad. Not only in her heart and mind, but clean down to the soul of her. She'd lie, she'd cheat, she'd kill to have her way. God alone knows how many men she's ruined."

"Her toboggan's traveling a lot faster than yours."

"I hope so. I sure do." She remembered the purpose of their meeting. "Bill, you've got to be on guard every minute. Cleve's probably told Gloria about your beating him up. They weren't speaking, but now they've made up. They went to bed together, I'm sure. Lord knows what kind of a tale he told her; whatever it was, it wasn't the truth. She's crazy about you and maybe he told her you are in love with Pat. You are, aren't you?"

"Are you loco?" asked Bill heatedly. "What in hell give you that idea?"

"You don't give a damn about women; if you didn't love her you wouldn't have beat him up for trying to touch her. You'd have raised that right eyebrow of yours and asked, 'Am I intruding?' and walked out."

"Discerning little wench, aren't you?" asked Bill angrily.

"I know my men. But whether you are or not doesn't matter. What does matter is that the two of them will cook something up between them, and now that Cleve's gunmen are back you'll have to wear eyes in the back of your head and keep them open all the time."

"Don't you worry none about me. You worry about Maybelle. If either of them finds out that you met me they'll raise hell with you. Better sneak back now before you're missed. Go on; run along."

"You'll be careful?"

"Sure. I always am. But I'm not running away from them. Best way to avoid a trap is to walk in and tear it apart before they get it set. Now get along with you. But before you go, honey, I'd like to kiss you. Just once."

She raised her lips and he pressed his against them. He said slowly, "That's the first decent kiss I've given a woman since my mother died."

"And it's the first I've had since Joe—Oh, Bill! If it wasn't for Joe I'd be damn' fool enough to fall crazy in love with you!"

"And I'd be complimented and mighty humble, Maybelle. Goodnight, kid."

She whispered "Goodnight" and moved across the range. She was like a wraith flitting over the turf and he watched her until the shadows swallowed her. His throat was tight and his eyelids burned. Too bad that she was so devoted to the memory of her Joe; she'd make a swell little wife for some lucky man. And yet he couldn't blame her; she was his kind. If he ever fell in love it would be for keeps, too.

He left with the same caution he had observed in coming, and when at last he reached the street he walked directly to the Silver Saddle and entered it. If there was to be trouble he'd rather it came now before they had the chance to set the stage and arrange the props.

Cleve Morley still stood at the bar. Gloria was seated at a table with Texas Tom and two other men. He had not seen them around since Thayer's cows had vanished and he guessed they were Swat Harrington and Harvey Short. They were both medium-sized men, but one had red hair and moustache and a freckled face and the other was dark and smooth-shaven and furtive-eyed. The four were talking and drinking. Gloria saw him and said something and the two he believed were Swat and Harvey got up and moved over to the bar.

Bill's lips tightened slightly. Maybelle's hunch was right; there was trouble coming. And it looked like the old squeeze play. He rather liked the idea.

When Cleve Morley had ridden into town from the Larkin homestead he didn't come down the main street but rode into the alley and directly to the stable. He was still seething with rage and humiliation. Not content with stealing Gloria from him, Bill Serviss had now appropriated Pat. Well, by God! He'd fix the fellow at both ends of the line. He'd queer him with Gloria by telling her about Pat and queer him with Pat by telling her about Gloria.

He automatically off-saddled and turned his horse into its stall, then crossed the alley and went up the covered stairway. Dusk had fallen and the bracket lamp in the hall was lighted.

He went to Gloria's door and got out his key with trembling fingers. He was fumbling with the lock when the door opened and Gloria stood looking out at him. Sight of his disheveled hair—his hat was still at the Larkin cabin—and his swollen and bloody lips, brought an expression of real surprise and shock to her face. She said, "For the love of God, Cleve, what happened?"

He pushed into the room and kicked the door shut behind him. She backed away before him and stood regarding him with the consternation still on her face. She said again, "Cleve, what is it?"

"Not pretty, eh?" he snarled. "Take a good look at it and start laughing. That bastard you fell for did it. Bill Serviss."

"No!" She was thunderstruck, not so much by the knowledge that Bill had meted out the punishment than that any man would have had the temerity to slap Morley around on his home ground.

"Out at the Larkin place," he went on savagely. "I've suspected Sam and his boy of rustling steers and thought I might pick up some evidence. I did. I found an ET hide. I told Pat about it and demanded that she tell me where they were hiding out. The little bitch started for a rifle and I grabbed her to keep her from getting it. She let out a squawk and Serviss came busting in like a mad bull. I had no idea he was around. He's four inches taller than I am and heavier, and he was mad and I wasn't. He laid me out before I even got started. It seems he's in love with Pat Larkin."

"In love with her? Bill Serviss? I don't believe it!"

"Oh, you don't!" Morley's sneer was the nastier because of his mutilated lips. "Well, maybe I can convince you. Of course, since you're so used to having men fawn over you, it may be difficult for you to believe that a man could prefer any woman to you; but what I saw should make it plain enough."

"What did you see?" Gloria's lips were tight and thin.

"I got on my horse and got out of there. I could have shot the bastard I guess, but after all if he thought his sweetheart was in danger I couldn't blame him for flying to her defense. So I got out. He stayed behind and after I'd ridden a short distance I got curious about what was happening in the cabin. I rode back and looked in the window. I saw plenty."

"Go, ahead."

"Want the details? Well, Serviss was standing on one side of the room and Pat had just come out of her bedroom. She had on a nightgown as thin as tissue paper. Something like the one you were wearing that night I dropped in on you and Bill."

"Okay, okay! What then?"

"What do you think? He let out a yell and started for her with his arms out like a starving man reaching for a T-bone steak. I didn't stay to see the rest. I didn't have to. My imagination's fairly good and it wouldn't have been sporting to stand there and watch, would it?"

She said tightly, "The lousy bastard!"

Her face was twisted into a mask of jealous hatred, but it remained that way only for a moment. Gloria was crowding thirty and about half of her life had been spent in playing percentages. Now she did some rapid calculation. Bill had fascinated her to the point where she had defied Morley, but now Bill was definitely out of the breadline and Morley spelled home and food and clothes and jewels. Her features softened and her lids drooped. Compassion came into the violet eyes. "You poor darling!" she murmured softly. "Bill Serviss never meant a thing to me. He scared me into going to his camp that night. There never has been anyone but you, dear."

It was food for his ego. The dog was back at his heel, contrite and repentant. "You haven't made any effort to prove it lately."

"I thought you were angry with me, darling. Here; lie down on the bed and let me fix your poor mouth."

He stretched out on the velvet coverlet and she got water and a face cloth and dabbed gently at the dried blood and purple lips. She wet a towel in cold water and put it over his mouth, first tenderly kissing the injured spot to make it get well. He grabbed her and drew her down.

When at last he left, she followed him to the door and pressed the cold towel into his hand. "Keep this on it, darling. And if you need me, call."

When she had closed the door behind him, she underwent another metamorphosis. Fury and thwarted passion came back into her face. Bill Serviss had treated her like a cur dog and he would suffer for it. She'd fix his clock and Cleve would be grateful to her for it. Cleve would stall along until he found a way to avenge the wrong without implicating himself, but she could not tolerate delay. She'd take the job off his hands.

How? She sat on the edge of the bed and thought up ways of removing Bill from circulation promptly and efficiently. She formed one plan only to discard it as inadequate or too dangerous to herself. She was still thinking it over when she went downstairs and entered the saloon.

And then she saw Texas Tom and had the answer.

She advanced quickly to him, a delighted smile on her face. "Why, Texas! How nice to see you back! Any luck?"

"Plenty." The look of a hungry dog was in his eyes and she could almost see him drool. "Gosh, honey, I'm glad to see you ag'in! I been dreamin' of you. How about a kiss, huh?"

"Why, sure." Gloria raised her lips and he grabbed her and crushed her close. For a second she surrendered herself completely, then pushed him away. "My, but you're strong, Texas! And what a kiss!"

"You ain't seen nothin', honey! I could show you the best time you ever had. I tell you I'm mad about you! What say, baby? Right now! Anywhere you say. How about it, hon?"

"Why, Texas, how you talk!" She was the shy schoolgirl now, blushing and avoiding his avid gaze.

"Come on, honey," he urged. "Come on!"

She looked up at him, her lids half closed. "What will you give me, Texas? I come high, you know."

"Anything you want! Any damned thing in the world! Jest name it!"

"You mean it?"

"Try me!"

"All right." She raised her lids and he saw that her eyes were cold and scintillating. She whispered tersely, *"Kill Bill Serviss for me!"*

For a moment it sobered him, but only for a moment. His face hardened.

"He been botherin' you?"

"Yes! I hate him! Kill him, Texas, and the whole night is yours!"

He drew in his breath, held it for ten seconds, then expelled it with a gusty sound. "He's as good as dead this very minute," he said flatly.

CHAPTER THIRTEEN

Yes, it looked like the old squeeze-play coming up. Two of them on one side of the room, one on the other. They'd maneuver Bill between them and two would get him into an argument and the other would shoot him; or the one would start the argument and the two would shoot. The key to the situation lay in figuring correctly who would do the shooting.

Bill had the clue to this. Maybelle had warned him of Gloria's vindictiveness and if Morley had told her about him and Pat he would have her undying hatred. Hell hath no fury, and so on. Texas Tom was playing up to Gloria and she could use her power over him to force him to do what she wanted. Texas Tom was elected to do the shooting.

It didn't take him long to figure this out and once satisfied in his own mind he proceeded to walk into the trap. One of the two at the bar had turned with his back to it, had hooked a heel on the rail and was glowering at Bill. It was the red-headed, freckle-faced man and he was clearly seeking a way of starting the argument. Bill decided to help him out.

He walked towards the fellow, but while he appeared to be glaring at him he could see Texas Tom in the back-bar mirror. He saw Tom get quietly to his feet, wave Gloria back and stand, slightly crouched, by the table. Bill halted before the red-head, but in a position that enabled him to keep Texas in sight.

Anticipation had hushed the crowd; they had sensed approaching drama and were watching in tense silence. Bill noticed that the faro dealer, who had been between him and

Texas Tom, had slid away into obscurity. The set-up was an old one and he probably knew what was coming. Or thought he did.

Beyond the end of the bar stood Maybelle. She was standing stiffly, her lips parted as though she would call a warning to him if she dared. He gave her the barest perceptible nod and she relaxed.

"You Swat Harrington?" Bill asked the red-head.

"Who wants to know?" The answer was as insolent as the fellow could make it.

"Ashamed of the name?"

"No, by Gawd! I'm Swat Harrington, all right. Who the hell are you?"

"Bill Serviss. I'm looking for the thieves that ran off fifty head of ET stock. You were missing about the time they disappeared; where were you?"

"Why, damn your soul! You accusin' me of rustlin'?"

"I'm asking where you've been for the past week or so."

"I been prospectin'! Anybody could tell you that."

Harvey Short turned to face Bill. "I'm in this with Swat; I was with him. We was prospectin' like he says."

"Can you prove it?"

"I can prove it!" said Texas Tom from the other side of the room. "I was with 'em."

Bill give him a swift glance. In that glance he gauged the distance and angle of fire. "I'll get around to you later," he said, and turned back to the two before him. "Bring anything back to show for your prospecting?"

"None of your damned business!" blazed Harrington. "If you figure we was rustlin', come out and say so."

"All right," said Bill promptly, "I'll come out and say so. I think you're a pair of lousy rustlers."

They both made as though to draw their guns, but the movements were not swift or certain; they were bluffing him to draw his own Colt, thus giving Texas the excuse he needed for shooting Bill in the back.

Bill gave him the excuse, but he didn't get shot in the back. His gun came out like a streak of light and he spun on the balls of his feet as he drew. He turned to the right and the gun whipped around with the movement and he fired as Texas was raising his .44.

He did not hesitate an instant; he wheeled right back and leaped away a yard or so and the two at the bar found his gun menacing them. He gave just one fleeting glance at the mirror and saw Texas Tom sagging downward, then his attention returned to the men before him. They were staring foolishly, their mouths open. The swiftness of the thing had stunned them.

"It didn't work," he told them coldly. "That trick's so old it has whiskers on it. Now empty your pockets on the bar and we'll see what you got to show for your prospecting."

They looked at each other, licked their lips and glanced towards Morley. Cleve came forward, said, "It seems to me you're going a bit strong, Serviss. You have no right to accuse men like this, and you'll have to answer for shooting Texas."

"I'll answer to nobody for what I do," said Bill. "Texas and these two polecats had me framed for a ride to the Hereafter. Everybody in this room saw Texas draw. They must have had a reason for wanting me out of the way. Maybe they thought I was getting wise to them."

Morley stared at him. "After what you found on the Larkin homestead, I should think you'd be out looking for Sam and Jimmy instead of hanging around town."

"Two men didn't drive fifty cows through the hills. They had to have help and these men were absent at the time." He spoke to Harrington and Short. "Go on; empty your pockets on the bar."

They complied reluctantly and with much mumbling of threats. Bill looked at an assortment of tobacco sacks, cigarette papers, matches, pocket knives, chewing tobacco, string, some dirty scraps of paper, a couple of gold pieces and some silver change. He sniffed in disgust. "No dust, no nuggets. All right; put the stuff back into your pockets. I still think you're cow thieves but I'm not going to arrest you yet. And if you have any ideas about carrying out those threats, take a look at your pal over there and think again."

He backed to the doorway, watching them, catching sight of Maybelle over their shoulders. Maybelle held her clasped hands overhead and was shaking them in token of congratulation. Everybody was watching him but Texas Tom. Texas was lying on the floor watching the ceiling without seeing it. He was very dead. Beyond him stood Gloria and at the moment she wasn't a bit beautiful. She looked like a haggard old witch.

Bill got on his horse and rode to the Larkin homestead. It was late when he reached it and the cabin was dark. He rode down to the corral. It was empty. He went to the rear door of the cabin and found it unlocked, and he knew even before he went inside that Pat had gone. He went through the place thoroughly, lighting a lamp and carrying it about in his search. He found not a thing to indicate that the Larkins were rustling, but he hadn't expected to because they would keep the truth from Pat. Her rifle was gone; she had taken it with her.

He got back on his horse and struck out for the hills, following the easiest route as she would have done. He wanted to overtake her, for if she knew where her father and brother were hiding he could follow her to them. He rode through the night knowing that she would do likewise, and he dismounted occasionally to examine the trail for prints. He found them easily, for she had not tried to hide them. Before morning came he knew that she was just roaming around without any destination, following the beaten paths through the hills.

It was after dawn when he found her. He smelled the smoke of her fire and it led him to her. She was kneeling by a fire poking at bacon in a skillet and at the sound of his approach she straightened and reached for the rifle which leaned against a tree. As recognition of him came she dropped her hands in a despairing gesture.

He dismounted. "It's my time to furnish the breakfast," he said quietly. "Sit down and take it easy; I'll have something ready in a minute."

She said nothing, just moved to a stone and seated herself dejectedly. She walked stiffly and he knew she was saddle sore. He spread a blanket on the ground under a tree and said, "Try stretching out for a spell."

She obeyed him apathetically, lying on her side and watching as he prepared the meal. She had fetched a plate and tin cup and knife and fork and he put beans and bacon on the plate and filled the cup with coffee and took them over and put them before her. Then he filled his own plate and cup and sat cross-legged opposite her. She ate slowly at first, then hungrily.

He said, "So you don't know where they are after all."

"I told you I didn't."

"When you're finished you're getting on your horse and riding back to the basin."

"No. I'm going with you. If you find them I want to be there." She looked at him directly and he remembered what Maybelle had said about her eyes being honest eyes. She added, "To help them if I can."

"You won't be with me when I find them. I could lose you in ten minutes if I wanted to. If you go on without me, you'll wind up by losing yourself. There's no sense in that. You're going back."

She looked steadily at him and he could not guess what was going on in her mind. After a moment she said, "All right. I don't suppose I have much chance of finding them alone." She pushed back her plate and sat looking down at the folded hands in her lap.

He warned, "And keep a gun handy."

He cleaned up the dishes, packed them, saddled her horse for her. He helped her mount. "Keep west by the sun; you should hit the basin before dark."

No goodbyes were said. She rode slowly away and he waited until the sound of hoofs had faded, then mounted and pushed on into the hills. An uneasy feeling that he was being followed rode with him, but after backtracking several times he shrugged it off. The only ones who had any reason for following him were Swat and Harvey Short and they had no means of knowing where he was. Unless, of course, they knew where Sam and Jim Larkin were hiding and were watching him in case he found them. He kept on, alert and on guard against a sudden attack, and by noon he had reached the flat with the ravines debouching upon it. It was here that he had lost their tracks when it had rained.

He investigated each ravine in turn, following it until he was sure that no horse had traversed it since the deluge. He finished with three of them that afternoon and made a dry camp for the night. The feeling that he was being followed persisted and he took precautions against surprise, bedding down on the top of a huge boulder where they could not reach him without giving warning of their approach.

In the morning he started on the fourth ravine, finished his investigation before noon and tackled the fifth of the six ravines. Its bottom was stony and hard but there were occasional patches of earth deposited by the subsiding water. On one of these he saw a faint hoofprint, moved ahead a few paces and saw another made by the same shoe. The gunnysack with which that foot was wrapped had worn through sufficiently to leave a mark. He was on the right trail at last!

He camped, ate a sparing dinner and pushed on. The ravine petered out in a growth of timber and he threaded his way among the trees, peering keenly about him. The timber thinned, came to an end, and he found himself looking down a rocky slope at a rough shelter. He saw a thin line of trees and brush and caught the sparkle of water through them. There was nobody in sight, but his range of vision was partially blocked by a ridge of rock some hundred yards down the slope.

Bill dismounted, tied his horse to a tree, took the glasses and moved ahead on foot, keeping the rocks between him and any watcher below. He gained the rocks, found a crevice through which he could look and levelled the glasses. Two men were working on the bank of the creek and the powerful glasses brought them right in front of him. They were Sam and Jim Larkin and they were washing dirt through a sluice box. His lips tightened; maybe they were prospectors—when they weren't busy rustling cattle!

A sudden drumming of hoofs brought him around to stare. Angling down the slope at a full gallop was Pat Larkin. She was crouched over in the saddle, her dark hair streaming behind her, her gaze fixed on the shelter below.

He swore and started running up-hill towards the tree where he had left his horse. Damn the girl! She hadn't gone back to the cabin; it had been she who was following him the whole time. And she had seen the camp and had known what it meant and had seized the opportunity to beat him to them. His anger grew but with it was mixed admiration. What a girl! Loyal to the core and ready to fight like a tigress for the ones she loved!

His anger was redoubled when he reached the trees. His horse was gone. Pat had been smart enough to turn it loose or move it before starting for the camp. He decided that she had not taken time to move it, but had simply turned it loose and sent it on its way with a slap on the rump.

He barged through the timber following the trail of broken brush and finally found the animal cropping the sparse grass in a little hollow. He walked it down without much difficulty, but precious time had been lost. He mounted and raced back through the trees and down the slope.

There was confusion below him. The two men were saddling their horses with Pat feverishly helping. He lunged on recklessly, wondering why they did not fire at him. He was close enough to recognize them now. Sam had finished saddling and was on his horse, riding around in short, nervous circles, urging the boy to greater speed. Jim's horse became nervous and refused the bit which Pat was trying to force into his mouth and the boy ran up to help her. The horse reared and struck out with its front feet. Jimmy sidestepped quickly, but the rein was jerked from Pat's hand and the animal wheeled and ran.

Pat screamed, "Take mine, Jimmy! Take mine!"

"And leave you with him? No!" His rifle had gone with the horse; he drew his sixgun and wheeled to face the charging Bill.

Bill pulled to a stop and raised his Winchester. "Drop it!" he ordered.

Jimmy yelled, "Get him, Dad!"

Sam raised his rifle, lowered it again. "I can't do it, son." He dropped the Winchester and got from his saddle, putting his hands into the air. Jimmy looked at him, swore and threw his Colt to the ground.

Bill said, "Keep your hands up. You're both under arrest."

He saw Pat give him one long despairing look, then sink to the ground and cover her face with her hands. She had gambled and had lost, and suddenly he pitied her.

CHAPTER FOURTEEN

He rode slowly down the slope, keeping his rifle in a position where he could flip it up and fire in an instant, guiding his horse with his knees. Sam stood dejectedly, his weary face turned towards his daughter; Jimmy was tight-lipped and defiant.

When Bill halted before the group Jimmy said, "What are you arrestin' us for? Where's your warrant?"

"I'm arresting you for rustling ET steers. This Winchester'll do for a warrant for the present."

"You can't arrest us without evidence. We had nothin' to do with the rustlin' of Thayer's steers or anybody else's."

"The evidence is in the safe at the marshal's office in Pandora. It's that fresh hide you put in the lean-to the other night. Thayer has identified it as coming from one of the stolen animals."

A look of amazement came into the boy's face. "A fresh ET hide! One that I put——! You're crazy! I haven't bought a hide from Ed Thayer for months and I haven't stirred off this claim since we left the basin. Ain't that so, Dad?" He turned to his father for corroboration.

Sam was staring at Bill also. He shook his head. "That's right, Serviss. I knowed you suspected us and I reckon I couldn't blame you none. We snuck away and tried to cover our trail so's we could work without bein' bothered, but we never rustled no steers."

Bill listened skeptically. He had heard guilty criminals make more convincing denials than this. One couldn't expect them to confess when a confession meant a halter around the neck.

He said, "Can you get anybody to testify that you haven't left here at any time during the past week?"

"Of course not," said Jimmy. "We've been here alone."

"Then you can save your story for the court."

"That hide was planted!" declared Jimmy heatedly. "We didn't steal any steers. We don't have to steal now that——"

"Jimmy!" interrupted his father sharply.

Bill was not impressed. "I'm no judge and I'm no jury; I'm just the ranny who does the arresting. Step over to one side, away from your guns."

Sam obeyed wearily; for a moment it looked as though Jimmy would leap forward and tackle Bill with his bare hands, then he strode angrily to join his father. Bill picked up the Colt and Winchester from the ground and took Sam's .44. He told Sam to catch up Jimmy's horse, and while he was about it tucked the two sixguns under the lashings which held his sougans and put the rifle across the limbs of a tree. When Sam returned with the horse, he took the Winchester from the saddle and parked it with the other one. "We can pick them up later," he said. "You men will ride ahead, taking the shortest route to Pandora. Pat will ride beside me. I'm warning you not to make a break."

Pat got up from the stone to turn a tear-streaked face to him. "They're not guilty. I know it. If you had any heart in you, you'd scc it, too."

Bill said shortly. "Even if I thought they were innocent there isn't anything else I could do. My job is to arrest suspects when the evidence warrants it."

She looked at him helplessly, hopelessly, then pulled herself into the saddle and followed her father and brother up the slope. Bill dropped in on her left side, keeping his horse a foot or two behind hers, reminding himself that the female of the species is often deadlier than the male.

It was mid-afternoon when they started, and dusk overtook them long before they had reached Pandora. Bill ordered them to lead the way to a good camping place and Sam found a little tree-filled hollow where there was water. Bill handcuffed each of the two men to a sapling, then searched them for weapons. Both carried knives which he appropriated. Pat stood at one side watching, her eyes smoldering, her face very white.

Bill walked to Pat's horse and took the rifle from its sheath. "I'll take care of this for the time being," he said. "Stake out the horses while I get supper, and if one of them gets away it'll be a Larkin who walks."

He paid no further attention to her, starting gathering wood for a fire, and after a short stubborn pause she picked up the reins and led the animals away. He cooked a good supper, taking his time about it. He filled Pat's plate and cup and took them to her, then served Sam on his own utensils. "Jim and I will eat when you two finish. You'll have to manage the best you can cuffed to those trees."

He went over to the fire and rolled a cigarette, and Pat promptly carried her plate and cup to Jim. He refused them at first, but she coaxed him to eat. Sam ate stolidly, hopelessly. When he had finished, Bill took the plate and cup, washed them and filled them for himself. Pat took Jimmy's utensils and ate sparingly.

When Bill had washed up he said, "You'll have to sleep cuffed to the trees." They were about four inches thick and he knew the men could not break them. "Pat, you have your blankets; you can sleep by the fire." He took his own bed back some distance into the trees, set that mental alarm clock which enabled him to awaken at any time he had fixed his mind on and promptly went to sleep.

He awoke two hours later and, as was his habit, lay there listening before making a move. He raised himself quietly and looked towards the fire. It had burned down to a small bed of coals and there was not much light, but he could see that Pat was not in her blankets. He got his Colt, rose silently to his feet and circled, treading carefully.

With the firelight out of his eyes he could see the tree where Sam was cuffed and the black blot which he knew was Larkin. He glanced towards the other tree some twenty feet distant from Sam's. There were two black blots there. Evidently Pat was talking quietly with Jimmy. Hatching something up?

Bill started for them, striding rapidly but as silently as he could in his stockinged feet, and one of the figures straightened and wheeled and he knew by its shape that it was Pat. She asked breathlessly, "Can't I speak to my brother without interference?"

He said, "Yes," and stepped past her. He ran his hand over the trunk of the sapling, turned and said, "Give me the knife." She had been whittling away at the tree with what must have been a small pocketknife.

She said, "No!" and faced him defiantly.

His voice was hard. "Listen, sister. I didn't subject you to the indignity of a search, but don't think I won't if you drive me to it. Give me that knife."

She turned and her arm moved in a throwing motion and he heard the rustle of brush where the knife fell. He said, "Thats just as good," and examined the tree again. She had cut a notch about an inch deep, but it would have taken three men to break the sapling. He said, "Go back to your blankets and don't let me catch you out of them again or I'll tie you, too."

Jimmy said, "You low-down skunk!"

Bill paid no attention. He examined Sam's tree, found it untouched by the knife, and went back to bed. He had quite an arsenal with him, his own Winchester and Colt, the rifle he had taken from Pat and two sixguns belonging to the men. He had run a saddle string through the trigger guards of the captured weapons and since he was using the saddle for a pillow he was quite sure that Pat could not get one without awakening him.

He woke again at midnight and made a round of the camp. Sam and Jim were both sleeping; Pat lay awake on her blanket staring up at him. He could not see her distinctly but a moonbeam fell over her face and the hazel eyes regarded him with smoldering hate in them. She did not speak; evidently she had decided that any further plea was useless. He felt strangely dejected as he went back to his bed.

He made another round at two and was awake and up with the dawn. He started a fire at once. Pat got up, rolled her blankets and laid them aside, then started towards the trees. He said sharply, "Where are you going?"

"To—to wash." She did not look at him directly and he grinned inwardly. He said, "Fill the coffee pot while you're at it." He walked over and gave her the coffee pot and went back to work. He got the fire going, waited until it had burned down a bit, then put the skillet on and sliced some bacon to fry. He remembered her then and turned to look in the direction in which she had disappeared. She was just emerging from the trees, holding the coffee pot in her left hand. She walked quickly towards him, stopped short six feet away.

He said impatiently, "All right; hand it over. I won't bite."

Her right hand came from behind her and he found himself looking into the muzzle of a .44. Her face was tense and her eyes glinted. She said, "Put up your hands and turn around."

It was not hard to figure. She had slipped around to his bed and had taken one of the captured guns. He stood looking at her, trying to read what was going on in her mind. She went on, "I'm not fooling, Bill. The gun is cocked and if you make a move I'll pull the trigger. I can't miss."

That was quite true, especially since she had worked herself up to such a pitch that reason had fled. His Colt was in its holster and there were few men who could match him in the speed of his draw, but an attempt to pull that gun would most certainly be fatal.

She said, "Don't force me to kill you, for I surely will if you don't do exactly as I say. Put up your hands and turn around."

Bill raised his hands shoulder high and turned slowly. She said, "Higher!" and he extended them the full length of his arms. He felt the tug at his side as she removed his gun. She said, "Now get the handcuff key and drop it where I can see it."

He said, "No can do. I don't have it on me."

"You lie! Turn out your pockets, one at a time."

He did this carefully and slowly, dropping the contents at his feet reversing the pockets so that she could see he had skipped nothing. Sam and Jimmy watched tensely from their trees. When the last pocket had been turned Jimmy called, "He's got it hid on him, sis. Make him strip."

Bill had turned to face her. He said, "I'd like that. Want me to?"

Her lips tightened. "Yes."

He pulled off his chaps and tossed them to her. She kicked them over to Sam and told him to look through them, not once taking her gaze from Bill. He drew off his boots then peeled off his shirt. They in turn were kicked over to Sam. Grinning crookedly at her, he shucked his pants. Sam reported, "Nothin' yet." He had even examined the gun belt and holster.

Bill wiggled out of his undershirt, tossed it at her feet and grinned. "Drawers and socks too?"

Pink crept into her cheeks, "Just the socks."

He sat down and removed them. Sam said wearily, "Nothin' in any of his clothes."

She said, "Sit right where you are," and backed away to where he had his bed. She was completely mistress of the situation. She went over his sougans, examined his saddle, looked around on the ground. She came back, her face a bit desperate. "You've hidden it."

"That's right."

"Get it for me or I'll shoot."

"You'll have to shoot. I'm not going to give you that key, and if you shoot me you can't find it."

"Just give me that knife of his," said Jimmy. "I'll soon cut through this saplin'."

Her face brightened. "Of course!" She backed to where the contents of Bill's pockets lay and picked up the knife. She had to put down the gun she had taken from Bill in order to do so, but as soon as she had tossed the knife to Jimmy she snatched it up again. Her features were animated now. She taunted, "You should have tied me, too."

"Yeah, I reckon I should," he said grudgingly. "But you're only postponing things. I'll get after you as soon as you leave, even if I have to walk. And I'll get you sooner or later."

"We'll take the chance." She was almost gay.

He said glumly, "Do I sit here all day in my underpants?"

"No, you may dress. Throw him his clothes, Dad."

A wad of clothing sailed through the air and Bill caught it. He wriggled into his undershirt and shirt, then stood up and put his legs into his pants. He bent down and picked up the leather chaps, flipped them out in front of him to straighten them, then suddenly tossed them right into her face. And immediately after them leaped Bill.

Pat staggered back a step and the gun she had cocked exploded. The bullet grazed Bill's sleeve but he was on her before she could fire again. He wasn't a bit gentle about it: he seized her wrists and wrenched and she dropped the guns with a little cry of pain and despair. Jimmy was wrenching at the handcuff chain, trying to reach her; Sam watched with flaming eyes. Bill tripped her neatly and she hit the ground with a thud. She sat there in a huddle, crying.

He backed away, picked up his Colt and returned it to its holster, then kicked the other gun towards his bed. He pulled on his chaps, buckled them, fastened the gun belt into place. He said, "And now, if there are no more interruptions, I reckon we'll get breakfast. I see you dropped the coffee pot; you should have held on to it. The handcuff key was in it."

CHAPTER FIFTEEN

THERE WAS NO trouble after that. When they resumed their journey Pat sat slumped in her saddle, her courage gone. Jimmy rode stiff-backed, his face flushed with anger and frustration; Sam was apathetic, a beaten old man.

They did not stop for dinner; it was too much of a job to shackle the men and keep an eye on Pat and at the same time try to cook something to eat. They pressed on and entered Pandora just before sundown.

Their entrance made something of a furore, for the news of the hide which had been found on the Larkin homestead had spread and wagers had been made for and against Bill's fetching the Larkins in. The fracas in the Silver Saddle, when Bill had turned the tables on the three who had sought to trap him, had also been broadcast and people eyed Bill with respect as he rode down the street behind his prisoners.

Pat's attitude changed with their entry into town; she straightened in the saddle and held her head high. Jimmy returned the glances of the observers defiantly, Sam remained beaten. He had lost every gamble he had ever made and had already conceded defeat in this one.

Morley came out of the Silver Saddle and walked along the sidewalk abreast of them, and Pink Paradine, the marshal, strode along with him. At the jail Bill halted his party and ordered the two prisoners down. Paradine ushered them inside and Bill unfastened the weapons he had collected and followed. When Pat would have gone in also he stopped her.

"We're going to question them. We don't want you around. Go hunt up a lawyer for them."

"There isn't a lawyer within a hundred miles," she said bitterly.

"That's too bad. They're entitled to one and they'll sure need one. But you can't come in. Wait over at the justice's; we'll be taking them over there for arraignment."

He went into the office and closed the door behind him.

Morley had entered with the marshal, but since he was a member of the Association which had hired him, Bill did not object to his presence. The Larkins were seated and Paradine watched them from a standing position against one wall. Morley was seated at Paradine's desk.

Bill said to the marshal, "Get that hide."

Paradine got it from the safe, spread it out on the floor. Bill said, "About a week ago I searched your place, Sam. I found the pile of hides in the lean-to and went through them. They were all old and had been tanned. Four or five night ago I was camped near your cabin in case you came back and I heard somebody open or close the door to that lean-to. He got away and I wasn't close enough to recognize him.

"Cleve Morley went to the cabin the other day and found this hide in the pile. Since it wasn't there when I looked I figure that the one who came to the lean-to that night must have put it there. You say it wasn't you or Jim; who else would have any reason for doing that?"

Sam shook his head wearily. "I sure don't know."

"It wasn't me or Dad," said Jimmy tightly. "We been work-in' on that claim for nine or ten days; ever since we rode out of the basin."

"All you got to do is prove you didn't leave your claim during that time and I'll turn you loose."

"I tell you we can't prove it. We didn't see a soul the whole time until you and Pat came."

"Then you're stuck with a rustling charge."

"I tell you we didn't do any rustlin'!"

"You'll get a chance to prove it in court. If you don't do any better than you have this far, you'll both hang."

For the first time distress showed in Jimmy's face; distress and fear.

"But I tell you we didn't——!" He broke off helplessly.

Sam said, "Ain't no use, son. The deck's stacked ag'in us. It's been thataway all my life. And now, just when I thought——" He broke off.

"When you thought what?" snapped Bill.

"Nothin'. Just talkin'."

"Talking might help. For instance, I'm sure that you two didn't drive those cattle alone. Tell us the names of the fellers that helped you and you might escape the noose."

"I don't know who done it. That's God's truth."

"Could it have been Texas Tom, for one?"

"Texas Tom?" Sam was genuinely puzzled.

"Yes. You could name him just as sort of a starter. He can't contradict you; he's dead."

Sam shook his head slowly. "I ain't goin' to lie. If Texas stole them cattle, me and Jimmy wasn't with him."

"No other names suggest themselves?"

"No, sir." Sam was sitting erect now and his watery eyes met Bill's without wavering. "I'm not lyin' about this business; I don't know a thing and I can't name a single name. That's the truth if I hang for it."

Bill eyed him keenly for half a minute. If this man was lying he was certainly doing a good job of it. He shrugged at last and said to Paradine, "Put cuffs on 'em and take them over to the justice."

They escorted the two across the street to the home of the justice of the peace. There was a small crowd outside his house and Pat was among them; they followed the prisoners inside and somebody went after the justice, who was hoeing his garden.

The justice came in wiping his hands on the seat of his pants. He tossed his hat into a corner, mopped his perspiring face with a blue bandanna, then called the court to order.

The hearing was brief. Morley testified that he'd found the hide in the lean-to and Bill told of the midnight visitor and his later discovery of the hide. He said that Thayer had identified it as belonging to one of the missing steers and would testify to that effect in court. Sam and Jimmy told the same story they had told Bill: that they had not stolen any cattle and had been working on their mining claim at the time the hide was put in the lean-to. The justice ordered them held for trial without bail and went back to his hoeing.

Bill helped Paradine escort the prisoners to the jail and lock them in cells, then went out to find Pat waiting for him. He said a bit testily, "What is it now? If you're trying to cook up another deal you'll have to see Pink Paradine. They're his prisoners now."

There was infinite scorn in her eyes. "You think you're awfully smart, don't you? Awfully clever! Because Dad and Jimmy were away from home so often you fastened on them as suspects from the start. When those steers were stolen right out from under your nose you got mad and hunted them down and pinned it on them to save your face."

"Sure," he said sarcastically. "It was much easier that way. Saved a lot of thinking and running around. I might as well come clean with you, Miss Sherlock. I stole the steers myself and planted that hide in the lean-to so's I could pin it on the Larkins. You just bet I'm smart!"

She was observing him steadily. "No, I don't think you stole the steers."

"Well, thank you! It's so——Hey! I didn't steal the steers but I did plant the hide; is that it?"

"How quickly you understand! You made a big point about my father and brother not being able to prove they were on their claim; can you *prove* that you didn't put that hide there yourself?"

Anger blazed up in him. "Why, you damned little—wench! I ought to wring your neck for that!"

"I'm sure you're quite capable of it; you're so brave when you're dealing with the weak and helpless."

"You really think I put that hide there?"

"Somebody did, I know that. I've lived with Dad and Jimmy all my life; I'd know if they were lying. They're not."

He studied her, meeting her honest gaze, for the first time doubting.

"If that hide was planted, somebody had a reason for planting it. What would that reason be?"

"Fear, probably. Fear that you were getting near the truth of who the real rustlers were. Everybody knew you suspected Dad and Jimmy; the real rustlers could plant that hide where you'd find it and clinch the case against them."

There was logic in that, he had to admit. And now he had asked the question, another answer occurred to him. Cleve Morley wanted Pat; suppose Cleve had planted the hide there to force her to give herself to him? He had bargained with her—or tried to bargain. The animal might have been destroyed and later found by one of Morley's men and the hide turned over to him. But that didn't fit; the man who had turned the hide over would know that Morley had planted it on the Larkin place—

He said, "I'll look into it. That's a promise. And if I find any reason to believe that the hide was planted, I'll see to it that Sam and Jim don't suffer."

He strode away still puzzling over the matter. The reason Pat had given for the planting of the hide stuck finally in his brain: somebody, knowing that Bill was getting close, had planted the hide to cinch the case against Sam and Jim. The names of Texas Tom, Swat Harrington, Harvey Short and Pink Paradine suggested themselves.

He went to the Silver Saddle in search of Swat and Harvey, intending to question them fully in regard to their whereabouts when the steers were stolen. They were not there. He made a circuit of the town looking for them and did not find them. There remained Pink Paradine, but as marshal of Pandora he would be something of a problem.

Bill found the marshal in his office; he had fetched supper to the prisoners and was waiting for them to finish their meal. Bill went directly to the point. "Paradine, were you with Texas and the others on their prospecting trip?"

"Nope, I wasn't. Things were quiet here in town and I just took a little time off to go fishin'."

"Where'd you fish?"

Paradine waved an arm in a vague gesture. "All over the place. Lots of mountain streams and all got trout in 'em. I like fishin', and I don't like to go to just one place and hang around. I ramble. I couldn't even tell you where I was from day to day." His face hardened. "Figure I helped the Larkins to rustle them cows?"

"You never can tell. It's my job to check on everybody. I've even checked on the men who hired me."

"Cleve Morley, too?" asked Paradine in surprise.

"Sure. One of the best ways to cover up would be to send for a detective—when the others were going to anyway."

"Uh-huh. Find out anything about Cleve?"

"Nothing to implicate him. I telegraphed Washington before I came out here on the job and learned that he has a contract for some two thousand head of beef to supply various Government posts and Indian reservations. I spent two days on his TV spread, one day in each of the two valleys. He was grazing about five thousand head on each side of that dividing mountain spur, which would give him just enough natural increase to fill his contract. The only rancher I have any cause to suspect is Cole Brent."

Paradine nodded. "I'd say he makes a good suspect. Don't belong to the Association and is mighty careful about lettin' anybody on his spread."

"You happen to know where Texas and the others did their prospecting?"

"No, and I don't reckon nobody else does. They got some place where they take out gold and they ain't tellin' nobody where it is."

"I'll damn well find out if I get hold of one of them. Don't know where they are, do you?"

Paradine said he didn't and Bill went out. He was dissatisfied with Paradine's fishing story but had no way of checking on it. He walked moodily up the street, saw Cole Brent sitting on the watering trough by the town pump and went over and stood looking down at him.

"Howdy, smart feller," said Cole.

"So I'm a smart feller! You must have changed your opinion of me."

"Yep, you're smart. Found two hand-made suspects and chased 'em right down and as good as got 'em convicted and hung. Rustlin' ring all busted to hell—in a pig's eye!"

"I take it you don't believe the Larkins are guilty."

"If they are, they're dumb as hell. What would be the idee in sneakin' down in the dead of the night to put that new hide right where you'd be sure to look? Don't make sense. But you was smart to grab 'em; they ain't got no way of provin' they wasn't down to that lean-to, and you'll get credit for hangin' 'em."

He spat a mouthful of tobacco juice at a lizard.

"That's the second time I've been accused of pinning it on the Larkins to save face," Bill said grimly. Then, suddenly, "Know anybody whose initials are J. P.?"

"J. P.?" Brent squinted thoughtfully at the ground. "Joe, Jim, John, Jack, Jake, Jeb——Know fellers by them names, but none of 'em has a last handle beginnin' with a P. Why?"

"My horse," explained Bill, "wears a small J. P. neck brand. He belonged to one of a pair of hombres who tried to ambush me a couple weeks ago. I planted him on the Larkin homestead and took his mount after they'd shot mine. If I knew who he was I might find somebody else beside the Larkins to pin it on."

"Still stabbin' around in the dark, huh?"

"That's right. What else can I do, with Sam and Jim Larkin playing hide-and-seek in the hills; Texas Tom, Swat Harrington and Harvey Short, going on a mysterious prospecting trip; the marshal of Pandora roaming around fishing; and a sour-puss of an old rancher who cuts loose with a rifle at anybody what sets a foot on his spread?"

Cole Brent grinned at him, and it was the first time Bill had seen him smile. "You know, I'm beginnin' to like you, Serviss. I'm kinda glad I didn't hit you that night."

Bill walked away, more disturbed than he was willing to admit. He intensified his search for Harrington and Short and failed to locate them. Nobody could, or would, tell him where they were. Had they been working with Sam and Jim Larkin, and now that the Larkins had been arrested, feared they would be implicated? Or had they vanished in the fear that Bill would force the truth from them and learn thereby that the Larkins were innocent? . . .

CHAPTER SIXTEEN

HIS UNCERTAINTY irked him; he was not used to uncertainty. The evidence against the Larkins was conclusive, but it was entirely too conclusive. And there were other things which helped shake his belief in their guilt—certain significant words uttered by Sam and Jim, Sam's utter simplicity and apparent honesty, Pat's belief that the evidence had been planted. Cole Brent's insinuation that Bill had taken the easy way out. Brent knew or suspected something and was following each movement with the eager interest of an adult watching a child trying to find its way out of a labyrinth. Brent wouldn't talk; he was having too much fun watching.

And who was J.P.? If Bill knew that he would probably have a decent clue to the mystery. Or, if he could round up Swat Harrington or Harvey Short. He had put the fear of God into them and he could make them talk. He went into the Silver Saddle once more in search of them.

It was still too early for a crowd and none of the girls were on the floor; but Morley stood at his place near the end of the bar and Bill went directly to him. "I'm looking for Harrington and Short," he said briefly. "Got any idea where I can find them?"

Morley was cold. "Not the slightest. I don't know what you want with them anyway now that your job is done."

"Who said my job is done?"

"I say it. You've found the rustlers and that's what we hired you to do. Let me have your bill and I'll pay you off."

"The Association hired me; they can tell me when I'm, finished and they can pay me off."

"I'm president of the Association and I tell you you're finished. And I'll pay you off and charge it to the Association."

"Two men didn't drive all those steers. I want the rest."

"I don't believe you understand. I say that as president of the Association I'm satisfied that you've finished your job."

"Get a statement in writing to that effect from the other members and I'll step down. Until you do that I'm still on the job." And he turned on his heel and went out of the place.

How he would have liked to hang something on that arrogant bird! But Morley was absolutely in the clear so far as Bill could determine. Morley got rid of his entire yearly increase through Government channels and Bill had checked at both ends to be certain of the number of head supplied and the size of the herd which supplied them. With less than ten thousand head, Morley would be forced to buy or steal some cattle to fill his contract without cutting his standing herd; but Bill had tallied five thousand odd on each side of that dividing spur.

He went down to the jail once more. Pink Paradine had just come out of the cell room with the tray of empty dishes. Bill said, "I want to talk to the prisoners again; let me have the cell keys."

"I'll go along and let you in."

"I want to talk to them alone; they may say something worth listening to if there are no witnesses."

Paradine scowled at him. "Reckon I'll listen in just the same."

"Reckon you won't. They're my prisoners, not yours. You're king of Pandora but on the range I'm the boss man. Let's have those keys."

Paradine surrendered them surlily and Bill went into the cell room. He turned at the doorway and said, "Better take back those dishes while I'm here to watch." He waited until the scowling marshal had departed, then unlocked the door to Sam's cell and went inside.

Sam was seated listlessly on his iron bunk; in the adjoining cell Jimmy paced back and forth. Bill said, "Now, Sam, I want the truth. I want it because I'm not at all satisfied that you're guilty after all." Sam looked up with a start and Bill went on."Yeah, that's right. When I arrested you I was sure you were guilty, and as things stand I reckon you realize that you're as good as convicted if I stop here. But I never yet sent an innocent man up knowingly and the only way you can convince me that you really are innocent is to come clean."

"But I already told you——"

"I know the story. It's what's behind the story that I want to know now. Back there on the claim Jim started to say something and you cut him off. He said, 'We don't have to steal because——' Because why?"

Sam gave him a long look, then glanced at Jim. The boy had stopped his pacing. He said, "Don't tell him, Dad."

"Later," Bill went on, "you said that hard luck had always followed you, even now when you thought—thought what?"

Sam was studying him intently. After a moment he said, "If I tell you I'll be fixin' to lose—everything."

"If you don't tell me, you're fixing to lose your life, and I figure that's just about as close to everything as you can come."

Sam shook his head. "My life ain't nothin' compared to Pat's happiness." His eyes were steady, earnest.

Bill said, "If it's anything that'll affect Pat's happiness I'll give you my word it'll never be used. Will that do?"

"Yes," said Sam after a moment, "that'll do. Serviss, you're a hard man but I reckon you are honest. I'm goin' to tell you."

"Dad!" cried Jimmy.

"Hush up, boy. For once I'm gonna do somethin' that my hunch tells me is right. Where's that pink-faced marshal?"

"Gone with the dishes. Talk low." Bill went over and sat on the bunk beside Sam.

Sam said, "For years, off and on, Jimmy and me been prospectin', hopin' to find enough gold to give Pat the things she should have. We'd keep tellin' her that it'd be just a little while longer, that we sure were on to something big. And we never made the grade.

"We'd see the disappointment in her face when we had to tell her the claim hadn't panned out like we expected, although she was mighty quick to hide it and smile at us and wish us better luck next time. It got so we decided not to say anything to her again; to just work away and if we struck it rich it would come as a pleasant surprise instead of a disappointment.

"Well, we struck it at last. Or believe we have. Back there at that claim where you found us we uncovered a vein that's gettin' fatter and wider by the foot. But we couldn't tell her until we were sure, and we had to hide our trail to it because we ain't filed on it yet."

Bill said, "And that's why you kept it quiet when I caught up with you. Not having filed on it you were afraid I'd stake it out for myself."

"Yeah, that's it. You still can stake it out. You know where it is, you can go back there and look at it for yourself, although we've taken pains to keep that vein hid. And you can keep your mouth shut and let us swing for somethin' we never did and if it's as valuable as it looks you can dig enough out of it to keep you the rest of your days."

"What makes you think I won't?"

"Just a hunch, Serviss; a hunch that for once I can gamble and not lose."

Bill got up. "I'm going to ride out there and see for myself. If it's as promising as you say it is, I'm sure enough going to file on it." He saw the consternation that came into Sam's eyes and added, "*In Pat's name.*"

Sam reached up to grip his arm, his watery eyes bright. "You will?"

"Yes. She's had to suffer for it, it should be hers. You'll never know how much that girl has been willing to sacrifice for you two."

Jimmy was staring through the bars. He said in a subdued voice, "You mean what you say, Serviss?"

"I always mean what I say. And if this claim is what you represent it to be, it'll go a long way towards convincing me that that hide was planted in your lean-to. Anybody with a fortune in his grasp would be foolish to try to save a hide off a rustled beef, even if he was crazy enough to steal it in the first place."

Sam rose slowly to his feet, his hand still gripping Bill's arm. "Serviss, you save that claim for Pat and Jimmy, and if you can't find them that rustled Ed Thayer's steers I'll confess to doin' it myself. I'll say Jimmy had nothin' to do with it; that it was Texas Tom and some fellers I don't know that helped me. I wouldn't mind doin' it at all; I reckon it'd be just about the only thing I ever done to help either of 'em."

Bill shook the hand off his arm. "Cut out that kind of talk. You haven't been convicted yet. I've got several leads to the rustlers to run down yet. Swat Harrington and Harvey Short have disappeared, and they were gone when Thayer's steers were rustled. That's one lead. Two fellows tried to ambush me and killed my horse. I shot one of them and took his mount. He was a jasper of average build, brown hair worn long, blue eyes and a sweeping moustache. Common enough; but the initials J. P. were branded on the neck of the horse and I figure they were his initials. Know who it was?"

Sam pondered, frowning at the floor. "J. P. That could be John something, or Joe or Jim or Jake—Jake! Jimmy, what was the name of that feller worked for the TV? Jake—Peters? Porter?"

"Potter," said Jim, his eyes very bright. "Jake Potter. He forked a roan then, but he might have switched to a bay. He had brown hair and a big moustache."

Bill said, "Thanks. Keep it to yourselves and keep thinking. You might remember another J.P."

He went out, his face tight. Jake Potter, who used to work for Cleve Morley. Well, lots of men had worked for Morley from time to time. But it was worth looking into.

He locked the cell door and went into the office just as Paradine entered. Pink said, "I been talkin' to Cleve. He tells me you're through and that you ain't to be allowed to see the prisoners any more."

"I'm not through by a hell of a sight and I'll talk to the prisoners any time I want to."

"You will over my dead body!"

"That may very well be. I'd sort of like that. Now get the hell out of my way."

He brushed past Paradine and went outside. A strange excitement gripped him, an emotion which he had often felt when a case was approaching its climax. A hunch told him that he was on the right trail at last. He hadn't eaten since morning and he was hungry, so he went into the restaurant, ate a hearty meal, then got on his horse and rode.

It was late when he reached the Larkin homestead, and he found the place dark and the kitchen door unbarred. He assumed that Pat was staying in town to be near her father and brother. He put his horse in the corral and bedded down on one of the bunks. In the morning he cooked breakfast on the kitchen stove, ate hurriedly and set out again. He rode hard and reached the Larkin claim before dark. Postponing his supper, he made an examination of the claim.

The vein, as Sam had said, was well hidden, but he found it. And when he found it, he stared, for while he was no miner he knew that Sam had really struck it rich this time. Conviction came to him then; no man with such a discovery to follow up would bother with rustling cattle. He remembered Sam's anxiety to get away from the cabin; it was caused by the feverish desire to resume digging for gold. Bill was ready now to stake his life on the innocence of the two Larkins.

He thought it over while he prepared and ate his supper. They were innocent but the evidence against them was damning. And it could not be controverted without revealing the overwhelming reason they had for sticking close to the claim. And the claim was not registered and would be the legal property of anybody who filed on it. Until he could ride to the county seat and file in Pat's name he dared not mention its existence.

The Larkins should be freed and there was but one way of freeing them. He'd go to the justice of the peace who had bound them over and ask for their release on bail. He'd tell the old goat he'd found new evidence and wanted them free so that he could watch them. Yes, that was the way to do it.

He started back the next morning, made the Larkin cabin by dark and, since the place was still deserted, camped in the shack. The following morning he rode to Pandora and found the justice in his garden. He explained what he wanted but the justice shook his head stubbornly.

"I ordered 'em held without bail and that's the way it stands. I been notified that you ain't on the case anymore."

"The hell you have! Who notified you?"

"Cleve Morley."

"Pay no attention to him. Set bail and I'll see that it's paid."

"Nope." The justice went back to his hoeing. "You ain't on the job no more."

Bill cursed him for a stubborn old fool and went to the Silver Saddle. Morley was not in the saloon and Bill went up the back stairs and walked into his room. Morley, awakened by his noisy entrance, sat upright in bed.

Bill said, "I told you I'd not recognize any order from any one man to get off the job. I just told the justice I wanted him to set bail so I could turn the Larkins loose in order to watch them. I want an order to him from you saying it's all right."

"But it isn't all right," said Morley smoothly. "You see, you aren't on the job anymore." He reached for his clothes, took a folded sheet of paper out of a pocket and handed it to Bill. "Read this. I contacted the other members of the Association and got what you asked me to get."

He watched with a sardonic twist to his lips while Bill read the order. It was a formal notice to him that his services were no longer required, and that if he'd present his bill to President Morley, said President Morley would pay him in cash.

CHAPTER SEVENTEEN

BILL READ IT, seething with anger. Morley was determined to get rid of him, and the probable reason lay in their clash over Pat. But there might be another: Morley could in some way be connected with the rustling.

Up until now Bill had suspected Morley only in a negative sort of way, just as he suspected Ed Thayer and the other members of the Association, simply because anybody, no matter how well covered, could be guilty. Now it came to him that an enemy of Morley's might point to some significant facts which could easily be interpreted as indications of guilt.

There was the hide of the stolen steer; if Morley had planted it for the purpose of bending Pat to his will, there still remained the question of how it had come into his possession. Then there was the frame-up against Bill. That might have been promoted by Morley in an attempt to get rid of him before his investigations went any further. The disappearance of Swat Harrington and Harvey Short could have been the work of Morley, who could not trust the dull wits of his henchmen to the same extent that he trusted his own. And then there was—

Bill said suddenly, "Cleve, what ever became of Jake Potter?"

The man gave a start, quickly repressed, but not quickly enough to prevent Bill's seeing it. "Jake Potter? Never heard of the man."

"That's funny. He used to work for you on the TV."

Morley frowned a moment, then his face cleared. "Oh, him! Couldn't place him at first; but then, outside of my foreman, I know the ranch hands only by their names on the payroll. Potter hasn't been with us for over a year. I don't know what became of him. Why?"

"He was one of the two who tried to ambush me that day; the one I shot." He dismissed the matter as of no consequence. "Well, this seems pretty definite. I'm off the case altogether now, huh?"

"That's right. We're quite satisfied with your work and there's no need keeping you any longer."

"From now on I'm just a private citizen, no longer duty bound to work in the interest of the Association?"

"You've no longer any standing. Present your bill and I'll pay you."

"I'll have to figure it out. Give it to you later."

He strode out of the room, closing the door after him. As he started down the hall a door on the opposite side opened and he saw Gloria. There was no seduction in the look she gave him, she glared like a snake about to strike. "You lousy bastard!" she spat at him. "Why did you kill Texas?"

"I don't know. I should have killed you instead, you cheap floosie. Don't blame me for his death; it was you who brought it about."

"Me! Why you——!"

He slapped her face smartly, first with his palm, then on the other cheek with the backs of his fingers. "Shut your dirty mouth! You're so low-down you stink!"

He went on down the hall, her curses following him. He grinned mirthlessly; stir 'em up, that was the way to do it. Make 'em mad, so mad that they'd stop reasoning in their desire to get at him.

He went across the street to get his horse, which he had left outside the justice's house. Pat was coming from the direction of his garden, her chin high, her face white and set. There was a desperate light in her eyes and he guessed that she had been appealing to the justice and had had her appeal refused.

He wanted to talk to her, to tell her of the new developments and his change of heart, but he crowded the temptation out of his mind. It would seem like an apology for arresting Sam and Jim and he wasn't ready for that. Any officer in his position would have arrested them on less evidence. And he had little hope to offer her as yet.

Nor could he tell her about their rich discovery. Armed with that information she might attempt to have them released and some bastard like Cleve Morley would find the claim and file on it. No, that must wait. Damn it! He should file on it for her; but he hadn't the time now. He must find Harrington and Short and frighten the truth out of them.

Pat saw him and turned abruptly to avoid him. She hurried along the sidewalk and he did not follow her. She hated him, he was sure. That it had been his duty to arrest her father and brother would not count with her. With women, sentiment came first, duty after.

He got on his horse and set out in the direction of the Twin Valley ranch. If Morley had sent Harrington and Short away, he might have ordered them to the ranch as the safest place to hide. He didn't ride into the basin but stuck to the hills, circling to the mountain spur that divided Morley's range. He followed the crest of this to the slope which overlooked the ranch headquarters and here made his camp. He ate his supper, for it had taken him the whole of the day to make the long trip, then got out his glasses and examined the place.

He was looking for men and he saw them when they came out of the mess shack. He scanned each in turn, recognizing the ones who had helped bunch the cattle for his tally. Then he sighted one who had not helped but whom he had seen over the rim of the iron tank in the Larkin yard. He was the heavy-set, black-haired man, companion of the one he had shot.

Neither Harrington nor Short were among the TV crew. Bill watched until darkness fell, then curled up in his blankets and slept. The following morning he started back towards Pandora.

Pat was licked from the start, for there were bugs on the justice's potato vines and when she found him he was scraping them into a tin can filled with coal oil and muttering to himself. He said before she could even speak, "Don't ask me to release Sam and Jim on bail. I bound 'em over without bail and that's the way it's gonna stay."

"But if I promise——"

"No! Cattlemen's Association want 'em held that way and if I was to let 'em out Cleve Morley'd have my job in no time. Dang these pesky potato bugs! Steal a man's meal afore he even gets it out of the ground!"

She knew it was useless to plead, especially since she could see a particularly large batch of bugs on the plant he was about to tackle. She choked back her despair and turned away. She felt very helpless and alone.

As she emerged on the street she saw Bill crossing from the other side and experienced that strange thrill she always felt at sight of him. She hated him, she told herself, yet she was fascinated by him. He was so tall, so strong, so resourceful. And he had iron courage. He wouldn't flinch at a levelled gun; not even when he knew it was cocked would he cower. He was so unpredictable; he was quite capable of gathering her in his arms and kissing her right here on the street, yet he had walked out when she lay naked and helpless before him and had refused her when she had offered herself to save her father and brother. Anyhow, after the way he had upset her brave plan for rescuing them she hated him and would have nothing to do with him.

She turned abruptly and walked towards her boarding house.

She found Mrs. Wilkins, the widow woman who operated it, waiting for her. Mrs. Wilkins took one look at her tragic face and said, "No luck, honey? Now that's too bad. I was hoping the judge'd temper justice with a bit of mercy."

"There were bugs on his potato plants," said Pat dismally.

"Just like a man, takin' his spite out on an innocent! Tell you what, dearie; why don't you run down and see Cleve Morley? He's president of the Association and he's such a fine gentleman."

Pat smiled a bit grimly. Gentleman! She remembered Bill's scornful comment, "I wouldn't want to be one; I've known too many of them." She knew at least *one* too many. She thanked Mrs. Wilkins and told her that might be a good idea.

She went to her room, took off her bonnet and sat down by the window to crochet. She could sell all the fancywork she made and they'd need money for the lawyer and to keep her until her father and brother were free. If they ever were freed! The thought of their conviction brought tears to her eyes. She must save them! Perhaps she could make a deal with Morley.

She quailed at realization of the kind of deal he'd demand, but set her teeth determinedly. She didn't know so much about it, but it couldn't be so awfully bad. Lots of girls made their living by selling their bodies and appeared none the worse for it. Men sold their muscles and their brains; a girl had only her soul. But it couldn't be so wicked if you did it to save somebody you loved.

Why should she find Cleve's touch so repulsive? Why was she so reluctant to make the sacrifice to Morley when she had been so eager to make it to Bill? The pink crept into her cheeks; she must be very wicked to even contemplate such a thing with Bill or anybody else. Yet she must steel herself to make any sacrifice, any sacrifice at all, if it would save her father and Jimmy.

That afternoon she walked past the Silver Saddle, trying to see over the swinging half-doors. They were so tall that she could make out very little of the interior. Cleve would be in there, she supposed. He probably lived over the saloon. Somebody had said the girls lived there, too. She went on down to the livery corral, talked to her horse for a little while, then returned to the boarding house and her crocheting.

After supper she set out again. She would try to see Cleve; she would swallow her pride and appeal to him. Of course, he was mad at her now, but it wouldn't hurt to try. Dusk had fallen, but she went into the store and looked about until it was quite dark. Almost guiltily she walked down to the Silver Saddle. She could hear voices inside the place and the clink of glass and coin; the smell of whiskey and tobacco smoke reached her.

There was nobody in sight and she slipped up to the doors and pushed one slightly back. Through the crack she could see one end of the bar. A girl stood there gazing right at her. The girl was small and slim and dark and her eyes smoldered. She had a cigarette between her fingers and she was looking at Pat without seeing her. Looking, perhaps, into a past that was always present.

Pat made a little hissing sound and the girl started, blinked, and recognition came into her eyes. She glanced about quickly, then came to the door, pushed it open and said, "What are you doin' here, Pat Larkin?"

"I must see Cleve Morley. Where can I find him?"

"You can't come in here. Go around to the alley; there's a back door. I'll tell Cleve to meet you there."

Pat said, "Thank you very much," and moved away, and Maybelle stood staring at the spot she had been for a moment, then shrugged and turned to the back of the room. Cleve was at the far end of the bar and Maybelle told him, "Somebody to see you out in back."

"Who?"

"A lady. And I said a *lady*."

"Sure you'd know one if you saw her?" Cleve straightened his tie, set his hat at a cockier angle and moved toward the back door.

Maybelle hurried to the bar and spoke to the bartender. "Steve, you got somethin' dark to put around me? I want to sneak out for a minute."

"I got a poncho you can slip over you. That do?"

Maybelle said it would and he fished a black rubber poncho from beneath the bar and shoved it over to her. She said, "Thanks, partner," and put it under her arm and slipped through the doors. She put it over her head and its dark folds enveloped her. She ran along the passageway beside the saloon, stopped at the alley and crouched, listening.

Pat was saying, "But I know they're innocent, Cleve! You can manage it. They could escape, break jail! They'll never come back, I promise you!"

"Why should I help them?" came Cleve's cold voice. "I made you an offer before and you turned it down. Why should I move a finger to help now?"

"You said—you—wanted me." The words came haltingly.

"Of course I wanted you; wanted you bad enough to offer you a mansion and everything that goes with it. Maybe I didn't offer enough."

"It was—different—then. I didn't realize they might h-hang!"

"Different, eh? And now you're ready to reconsider?"

She said earnestly, "I'll do what you want me to, Cleve. Not go away with you; I couldn't do that because I must be with Dad and Jimmy. But I'm going to the homestead tomorrow. I just can't afford to stay in town. I—I'll be alone there, and if——" She was stumbling all about now—"If you happened to—to drop in, you'll find the door unbarred."

"Now you're talking!" There was passion in Morley's voice. "And your price is your father's and brother's freedom, eh? If I promise to get them out of jail I can come out, eh?"

"Y-yes. Yes, that's it." The voice was husky but brave, and Maybelle stirred angrily.

"Let's see if you really mean it!"

There was a short silence, then Maybelle heard Pat's voice, strained, broken. "D-don't, Cleve! You h-hurt!"

The answer was low, throaty. "You beautiful thing, you! I'll do it. Be at that shack tomorrow night waiting for me. If you disappoint me this time I'll take them out of jail and hang them myself!"

"I'll be there." She was almost crying. "I promise. Now I must go."

Maybelle didn't stop to hear any more. She fled up the alley, stripping the poncho from her as she ran. She pushed through the doors and slammed the poncho down on the bar.

Steve said, "What's eatin' you, cow gal? You look like you'd seen a ghost."

"Ghost, hell! It was the devil himself, Steve. The dirty, lousy bastard!"

CHAPTER EIGHTEEN

BILL HAD A REASON for returning to Pandora. A hunch kept riding him that he should file on the mining claim in Pat's name as soon as he could possibly do so, and to reach the county seat he must pass through Pandora. Then there was Swat Harrington and Harvey Short; believing that he had left this part of the country, they might return to town. And he was convinced now that in them lay the key to the whole situation. He knew he could handle them, that by being real tough he could scare the truth out of them. And nobody could be tougher than Bill Serviss when it suited him.

As he rode he puzzled over the matter, looking at it now with the assumption that Cleve Morley was the leader of the rustlers. His knowledge of the inner workings of the man's mind strengthened his suspicions; Morley was another of those "gentlemen" he had known who, beneath a veneer of polish and courtliness, was a cesspool of iniquity.

It wasn't Morley's attitude towards Pat that stirred Bill's animosity; or at least he told himself that it wasn't. Women were fair game. Like does, who were beautiful and graceful and soft-eyed and were spared only for the purpose of breeding more beautiful and graceful and soft-eyed animals for the hunter. He despised and hated the man because he knew that Morley would lie or cheat or steal or stab in the back if there was profit in it or if his security was threatened; and he was doubly damned because he hid his rottenness beneath a veneer of culture and refinement.

If Morley grazed less than ten thousand head of cattle the thing would be quite simple to figure out. He just couldn't go on supplying the Government with two thousand head a year without depleting his herd. That meant he would have to buy stock, which was not profitable, or steal it from his neighbors, which was. But Bill had himself tallied approximately five thousand head in each of the two valleys and a careful investigation had failed to reveal any outside sales by Morley. If he were stealing stock, he was disposing of it on the other side of the border. This would have to be proved, and proving it would be tough.

Something might be learned by tracing Morley's deliveries to the various Army posts and Indian reservations he supplied, but this also would be difficult. Bill had not attempted it because at first he had no reason to suspect Morley; now, he decided, he might have to do it after all.

It took him the full day to make Pandora and he rode at once to his usual camping place and cooked his supper. When he had eaten he lounged around smoking and resting. If Harrington and Short returned to Pandora they would not show at the Silver Saddle until later. Around ten o'clock he started uptown.

He kept to the shadows and entered the Silver Saddle with the assurance that his presence in town had not been reported. A quick glance told him that the two he sought were not there. He saw Morley at his end of the bar, he saw Gloria at the wheel with a half-drunken miner, and he saw Maybelle working listlessly on a cowpuncher from the ET. Morley gave him a stare, Gloria a scowl, and Maybelle a look of almost desperate appeal. He ignored the first two and sent Maybelle a quick, short shake of the head. At the moment he felt that he would be bad medicine for her.

He went to the bar and ordered a drink and asked Steve, the bartender who had slipped him Maybelle's note, whether he had seen Harrington or Short. Steve told him he hadn't. In the backbar mirror he saw Morley advancing towards him, but pretended not to. Morley stopped beside him, said in a low voice, "I thought you'd gone."

"Did you?"

"I told you you weren't needed around here anymore."

"Also that I'm a plain, ordinary citizen who doesn't have to take orders from anybody."

"A plain, ordinary citizen hasn't the privileges of a lawman, Serviss. He can be arrested and tossed into the clink."

"You haven't a man big enough to arrest me if I don't want to be arrested. Or two of 'em. Or a dozen."

"I don't want to throw my weight around unless you force me to. Frankly, I don't want you around Pandora. I'm not going to have you around. Is that clear, Serviss?"

Bill sighed wearily. "That's been clear for quite some time. Happens you and me don't see eye to eye. I'll stay as long as I want to and get out when I feel like it; so sic on your dogs."

Morley studied his fingernails for a moment. "You've had your warning," he finally said, and moved away.

Bill saw Maybelle approaching, gave her a warning shake of his head and turned away. Damn the girl, couldn't she see the way things stood, with Morley looking like the wrath of God and Gloria scowling at him from the roulette lay-out? He circled the room casually, keeping out of Maybelle's reach.

He passed Gloria and she hissed, "Bastard!"

He said, "Good evening, bitch!" and passed on.

He found a chair in a corner, sat down and tilted it against the wall. He pulled his hat brim down over his eyes so that he could watch without appearing to do so. He saw Gloria talking earnestly, fiercely to the miner. The man looked startled, glanced quickly at Bill, and Bill heard his raised voice say, "Him? Not me, lady!"

Gloria spat a vicious name at him and stalked away and Bill inwardly grinned. She had probably told the miner some wild tale and asked him to polish off Bill for her. It just happened that the fellow wasn't another Texas Tom.

Maybelle steered her cowpuncher to a place near his chair, got him interested in a black-jack game, then turned briefly and whispered, "Bill, I got to see you."

He said without moving his lips. "You crazy? I'm poison."

"It's important!"

"Come to the camp." He got up, stretched and yawned, and sauntered along the wall to the doorway and through it to the street.

There he stepped quickly out of the circle of light and stood against the dark wall, watching. Nothing happened. Satisfied that Morley had not yet turned his dogs loose, Bill moved on down the street, still keeping to the shadows. He went in a direction opposite to that of his camp, waiting until he was sure nobody was following before he cut across the street and retraced his steps.

He went to his camp, rekindled the fire, then moved back into the trees to wait for Maybelle. He smoked while he waited, not knowing how long it would be before she got a chance to slip away. He did not have to wait long.

She came gliding out of the darkness, her yellow dress hidden beneath a long, black poncho. She came right into the circle of light and stood looking about her. She said, "Bill!"

He said, "Over here. Out of the light."

She crossed to him swiftly, dropped down to sit on her heels, cow-country style. She said, "Bill, there's hell to pay. Know what the Larkin kid has done? Offered herself to Cleve Morley so he'll turn her father and brother loose!"

Bill almost swallowed his cigarette. "What's that?"

She told him swiftly. "I heard her. Last night. She came to the Silver Saddle lookin' for Cleve and I met her at the door. I sent her around back and told Cleve, then skinned out and ran back to the alley to listen. Bill, that dirty dog made a deal with her. She's to be alone at the Larkin cabin tonight and he's going out to stay with her. Goddam him! Bill, you've got to save that kid from him."

"You telling me?" Bill's face was tight. "Where's Morley now?"

"He just left. Told Gloria he had a headache. I don't think she saw me leave, but if she did and jumps me for it I'm going to tear into her. She's been like a wild woman for a week and, Bill, she'll kill you if she gets half a chance!"

"Maybelle, I'm grateful to you for telling me about Pat, but you mustn't take such chances. They'll murder you in a minute if they think you're passing information along to me."

"Let them!" Maybelle's voice was tight. "Let them! I'm tired of living anyhow, and if I go I'll sure take somebody with me. But you look after that kid, Bill. Promise me you will."

"Do you need my promise?" he asked soberly.

She shook her head. "No. You love her. I'm glad. Be kind to her, Bill; she's such a sweet kid. G'night."

She was up and gone before he could detain her. He didn't want to detain her; God knew she was in plenty danger as it was. He got up, rolled his bedding, then picked up his saddle and carried it to where his horse was staked out. He rigged the animal, coiled the picket rope, led the horse back to the fire and strapped on his bed, working mechanically.

His hands trembled with eagerness. The showdown with Morley had come. Damn his black heart! Bless the loyal girl who would sacrifice herself to save the ones she loved! He did not blame her; she was a woman and physically weak, but her heart was of tempered steel and she must use what means she had to buy the freedom of her father and brother.

He'd kill Morley tonight. He'd reach the homestead before Cleve and hide behind that iron tank and watch. Wait until Morley was about to sample the fruit of his victory and then jump him. He'd punish him first; beat him, maul him, tear off his limbs, gouge out his eyes! Punish him as only a tough ruthless man can punish!

He spurred out across the rangeland, taking the shortest route to the Larkin homestead. He rode hard and held the pace until the wind rushing by his face had cooled his brain and brought some semblance of reason to him. At this rate he'd exhaust the horse long before he reached his destination. He pulled down to a trail lope, took a deep breath and began to think clearly.

The deadly rage died and he saw that he couldn't kill Morley yet. He must first pin the rustling on him, strip the fine gentleman of his shoddy raiment and show him up for what he was. And if he merely beat him into a palpitating pulp, Morley would take his vengeance on Pat; she would never be safe from him and Bill could not remain to guard her. He must file on that claim and he must search for Harrington and Short. Reluctant as he was to postpone the pleasure of killing this poisonous reptile, he must find another way.

For Pat, the hour of execution was nearing. Execution because, no matter how she tried to argue or condone, she knew that after this night with Morley her soul would be dead. She would be defiled, dirty, and seared with the shame of it.

All the pure instincts which had been bred into her through generations of tradition and training rebelled against the thing she was about to do. To sell herself, no matter at what price, was wicked and degrading. To give—that was different; for she would give only to the man she loved. And to that man she had always resolved to surrender herself clean and untarnished. After tonight she could not do this. No matter whether or not he knew, she could never do it. Men could sleep with women and then go to the one they wanted for wife with clear consciences; with women it was different. Pat wondered vaguely about this and decided that it was the children which made the difference.

Children must be born untainted of a mother whom they could love and respect.

She ate no supper; prepared it and then put it away, her appetite gone. She tried to crochet but her fingers were all thumbs. She put up the work. Oh, why didn't he come and get it over with? It was midnight; he should have been here before this.

How should she greet him? She knew little about such things but she imagined he wouldn't want her to be wearing very much. That nightgown she had put on for Bill, the one she was saving for her wedding night, the wedding night that now would never come. Yes, she thought soberly, she must wear that. Her others were coarse, of muslin, fitting close about her neck. She went into her room and got it from the bureau drawer and spread it out on the bed. Revulsion overcame her. She wouldn't go through with it. She just couldn't! She crammed it back into the drawer and pushed it shut.

She ran to the front door and put her hands on the bar which fitted across it, then took her hands away and leaned weakly against the wall. She had to go through with it; the lives of her father and brother depended upon her. What was it Cleve had said? "If you're not there waiting for me I'll take them out of jail and hang them myself!" And he would! He was powerful, vengeful. He'd do just that.

She walked back into the front room and sat down on a chair. She sat rigidly, her hands in her lap. She didn't hear the beat of hoofs because of the deep sand, but she heard the horse blow when he was halted outside the cabin door. Dear God, he had come!

She heard the soft thud of boots diminish towards the corral and supposed Cleve was leading his horse to the enclosure. She went to the window and tried to see through it, but the room was lighted and it was very dark outside. The bar leaning against the kitchen wall called to her to come and put it into place; she started towards it, then with an effort of will returned to the chair and sat down. Her head was high; she had made her bargain and she would keep it.

She heard the footsteps approach the cabin. Somehow they didn't sound like Cleve's footsteps; they were bold footsteps, not soft, sneaky ones. Perhaps it was because he was so sure of himself tonight.

The latch rattled and she sucked in her breath and looked fixedly at the kitchen door. It moved inward suddenly and a man stepped into the room. He was tall and strong and his eyes smoldered. Her spirit rose like a lark on the wing. She sprang to her feet.

"Bill!" she cried. "Oh, *Bill!*"

He said, "Get into your riding clothes; we're clearing out of here."

CHAPTER NINETEEN

At that moment Bill was everything to Pat. He was God. Or the messenger of God, for he had saved her. Let Morley come now; he would not dare to touch her in Bill's presence, and it would not be her fault that her bargain with him was not kept.

She heard Bill say impatiently, "Don't stand there gawking! I said to get on your riding togs. We're getting out of here."

Her excited brain cleared. "But I can't! I can't!"

"Oh, yes you can. You are. You're not playing house with Cleve Morley this night."

Her cheeks flamed. "How did you know?"

"Never mind. Get into your riding clothes. Your horse is saddle and waiting."

Thought of Cleve's words returned to her. "But I tell you I can't! I've got to stay. If I don't, Cleve said he'd take Dad and Jimmy out of jail and hang them himself."

Bill's eyes widened, then narrowed. "He did? Well, he won't. Do you get dressed or do I have to dress you?"

He advanced threateningly and she retreated hastily towards the curtained-off bedroom. "Yes, Bill! I—I'll change."

"You have five minutes," growled Bill as the curtain fell behind her.

She changed hurriedly, troubled again. Bill had said they wouldn't hang and they were Bill's prisoners and she could trust his word; still uncertainty remained to torture her. She went out to find him pacing restlessly. He flashed her a quick glance, said, "Come on," and led the way from the cabin. He did not bother to extinguish the light. The horses were standing outside the doorway and he held hers while she mounted. She asked, "Where are we going?"

"To a place where you'll be safe from Morley. Then I'm coming back and finish up this case. And I mean finish it. I'm a free lancer now and take orders from nobody but Bill Serviss."

They were half across the basin before the significance of his words reached her consciousness. She drew rein sharply. "What do you mean you're a free lancer?"

He laughed mirthlessly. "Cleve convinced the Association that when I fetched in your father and brother I'd done my job. They fired me."

"Then you can't——! Bill, if you're out you can't stop Morley!"

"Who said I can't?"

"I say it! He'll do what he said!" She wheeled her horse. "I'm going back!"

He was too quick for her, seizing her rein and jerking the horse to a sudden halt. "Listen, you dumb, stubborn—*loyal* little brat! You're coming with me. If you don't come peaceably I'll rope you on your horse like a sack of oats. Now ride ahead and turn when I tell you."

Her eyes challenged his through the darkness, but in the end she reined her horse about and once more took the lead.

They rode through the night, Bill forcing a fast pace. She was saddle sore and tired, but he did not relent; and shortly after dawn they passed through a fringe of trees and came to a slope and Pat looked down at the shelter her father and Jimmy had erected on their claim.

They halted by the creek and she was so sore that she could not dismount. He lifted her down and carried her in his arms like a child into the shelter. There were two bunks and he placed her gently on one of them and straightened to look down at her. For the first since she had known him she saw warmth in his eyes, warmth and gentleness.

He said, "Take it easy and I'll rustle something to eat. Then I'm on my way. I'll take your horse with me; I don't want you riding back to mess up things. But your father and brother will not hang. Remember that."

She felt suddenly tranquil. She murmured, "Yes, Bill," and closed her eyes.

When he awakened her the smell of food was in the air. He said, "I've eaten and I'll be going now. Stay right here. There's plenty of grub and nobody will disturb you. I got the two rifles I hid in the trees and they're here. Take care of yourself!"

He stood looking down at her and she saw the hunger for her in his eyes. He dropped suddenly to his knees beside the bunk and leaned over her. He said almost gruffly, "Kiss me, Pat."

Impulsively, she turned her lips towards his, then remembered her promise never to return his kiss. At the last moment she moved her head and felt his hot kiss on her cheek.

He got up, said, "Some day I'll have your lips. Willingly. No other way will do."

He strode out and she heard him ride away.

He did not take her horse far; he could not be bothered dragging another animal behind him. He found a little hollow a mile or so from the cabin, saw there was grass and water, stripped the horse and hobbled it with rope. It would not stray far and must return for water. He hid the saddle and rode on.

He pushed the tired horse, realizing to the full, the need of haste. Maybelle had not told him of Morley's threat and its revelation by Pat had given him a jolt. He reasoned that nothing could have happened yet. It would have been two or three in the morning before Morley could have returned to Pandora after his visit to the cabin. He would sleep late. It would be noon before he could start the ball rolling.

How would he arrange to hang them? Call in the crew from the TV, possibly talking Ed Thayer's men into joining them. Rounds of whiskey and grumbling about lousy rustlers and the uselessness of a trial where the evidence was so conclusive. One or two well-paid men to inflame their passion, a sudden suggestion that they take the prisoners and hang them then and there. A half-hearted resistance by Pink Paradine to save face, then a surging mob to take the two from their cells and a quick hanging over the livery corral gate.

That was the obvious way, but Morley was anything but obvious. He was a gentleman; there must be nothing crude about the affair. How else? Bill thought he knew and he spurred the harder at the thought. He did not stop for dinner, watering his horse sparingly at a creek and then riding on. He crossed the basin, where the Larkin cabin stood, an hour after noon and sighted Pandora around four. He did not ride directly into town, circling and coming in from the range and halting behind the Silver Saddle stable and tying his horse there.

He stole past the stable, crossed the alley and made his way along the side of the saloon to the street. He peered cautiously around the corner. There was not a human being in sight, but in front of the store a hundred yards up the street he saw several buckboards and a whole rank of horses at the hitching rack. His face tightened; he had guessed correctly.

He slipped around the corner and looked through a window. The interior was gloomy but he saw there was but one person in the saloon. He moved to the doors and pushed through them. The lone occupant was Steve, the bartender, and he stood with his elbows resting on the bar and his chin in his hands and he looked gloomy. At sight of Bill he straightened, his eyes kindling. Bill asked, "Where's everybody?"

Steve jerked his head. "Down at the trial."

"In the store?"

"Upstairs. Hall there they use for dances and such-like. They're fixin' to hang the Larkins."

"I'll un-fix that."

Bill went out. He ran now. As he was about to mount his horse he halted with a foot in the stirrup. The animal was dead beat. He went into the stable and found a horse in a stall there. Probably Morley's. He hoped it was. He switched his rig, tossing his sougans into a corner. He rode around the town and approached from the other side. Behind the store barn he dismounted, tied the rein with a loose slip knot to a ring in the wall. He went in through the rear door, walked the length of the gloomy building and halted just inside the front doorway.

There was a lean-to behind the store which was used for storage and as a loading platform. He could see two open second-story windows above its slanting roof. No heads were visible, but voices came to him, one sharp and probing, Morley's, and the other weary and beaten, Sam's. He thought a moment, mind working ahead, forming his plan, then stole quickly to the back of the store and along one side to the street. He must have two horses and if there was a guard in front he'd have to get them the hard way.

There was. The entrance to the upper floor was through a doorway on his side of the building and up a flight of stairs, and as he cautiously put his head around the corner he saw a bent knee protruding from the doorway and part of a hat brim.

He retraced his steps, pushed open the big doors on the loading platform and climbed inside. He walked along an aisle with bales and boxes piled on both sides and could see through an open doorway into the store itself. There wasn't a soul in it. He went on through the store to the front door, peered around its frame, slipped outside and inched along the show window to the side of the upstairs entrance. He raised his gun high, said softly, "Hey!" and when a startled head popped out he hit it.

He hit it hard, not daring to take a chance, and the guard fell forward and right into his arms. He dragged the man off to one side, ran down the steps to the hitching rack, made a quick selection and untied two horses with TV brands. He led them around the store and back of the barn and tied them to the same ring where his own mount was secured.

He went into the barn and scanned the walls for what he wanted and found it. Two ladders, one long and one short, hung from spikes in the wall. He took the latter, carried it outside and set it gently against the eaves of the lean-to. He climbed it swiftly but silently, crawled up the slanting roof and crouched just beneath one of the opened windows.

Morley was saying, "And so Bill Serviss can prove that you didn't leave that mysterious claim of yours! Well, where is he? Where, by the way, is your daughter? Funny that she isn't here to lend her moral support, isn't it? And speaking of *moral* reminds me: I rode out to your place to tell her about the trial and she wasn't there. A lamp was still burning, but she was gone. Where is she? Or perhaps I should ask, where are *they?*"

Bill didn't wait any longer. He had never been inside the place but he could imagine the lay-out. At this end, in the rear of the building, would be some kind of stage; the audience would be out front. Proceedings would be conducted on or before the stage. He didn't give a damn; he'd play them as they fell. He stood up and in the same motion thrust his left leg through the window. His gun was drawn and levelled. He pushed forward and struck the floor with his foot. He pulled his right leg after him, stood erect.

He was on a low stage. Ahead of him and a bit to his right was a table with a chair; behind the table and on the chair was the justice of the peace, now arrayed in a threadbare frock coat. Before the stage Morley was pacing back and forth, and sitting stiffly on two chairs, wrists cuffed, were Sam and Jim Larkin. In another chair just one jump from them sat Pink Paradine. The spectators filled the chairs in the auditorium and lined its walls. Off to one side sat a group of men whom Bill assumed were acting as jury. Bill had a fleeting glimpse of the cold, sardonic face of Cole Brent in the audience.

All this in one quick glance, then the fireworks.

Pink Paradine, if not the first to see Bill enter, was the first to recover from his surprise. He came to his feet with a shrill yell, his chair going over behind him, and he was reaching for his gun even before he got under way. Swift he was, swift as the bullet that speeds to its target. And as sure, also. But Bill had him cold, for his Colt was already out and levelled. He fired and saw a round, dark hole suddenly appear in the middle of Pink's forehead. Paradine went over backwards as though smitten by a maul and he hit so hard that the rafters shook.

Instantly, Bill's Colt swept over to cover Morley. He had drawn the hammer again and his thumb was taut on it. He moved forward, said harshly, "Hold it, or Morley goes too!"

Morley had whipped around and was staring, his lips rounded as though the words "Don't shoot!" were about to emerge. Bill went on quickly, taking advantage of the consternation his action had caused. "Morley, tell 'em to stand hitched! They can get me but sure as hell is hot I'll take you along!"

Morley managed to gasp, "Don't—anybody—move!"

Bill's quick glance picked up Cole Brent again. Brent was grinning and his eyes glinted. He was enjoying the show.

Bill said, "I'll give my testimony now. Sam and Jim Larkin are in the clear. I know they were on their claim when the hide was planted. Morley had me taken off the case so he could vent his spite on them. Why? Because Pat Larkin refused to pay in the coin he demanded for the release of her father and brother Yes, she's gone. I took her to a place where she'd be safe from him. And now I'm going to take Sam and Jim. They're my prisoners, and if they come to trial it'll be before a real court and in the proper manner. If anybody tries to stop me I'll send Cleve Morley's dirty soul to the hell where it belongs."

There was silence for a moment, then he heard a harsh gasp and looked across the intervening heads towards a group of women near the back. They were Morley's girls and Gloria was among them. It was she who had gasped, and now she was standing, her face blazing with wrath, her hot gaze fastened on the transfixed Cleve Morley. Another of her men had gone sour on her; her breadline was crumbling.

Bill said, "Sam, Jim, come up here. Keep out from in front of me."

They got up, Jim's face bright, hope shining in Sam's tired eyes. They sidled along the wall and mounted to the platform. Bill said without looking at them, "Out the window and down the ladder. Horses behind the barn."

He heard their boots on the lean-to roof, waited until the vibrations of the ladder had ceased, then backed slowly to the window. Not for an instant did he remove his gaze from Morley's face, nor did his thumb relax on the hammer of the Colt. He saw Cole Brent stand up, his hand on the butt of his gun; but Brent was gazing sharply about the room and Bill knew that for some strange reason this gaunt, hard cattleman was on his side.

He slid through the window, going about it slowly and deliberately, not shifting his body and keeping the Colt aimed directly at the staring Morley. Both feet on the lean-to roof, he turned, slid down the incline and plunged to the alley below. He got up and ran to the barn entrance, turned to fling a pair of shots through the windows, then leaped into the building and raced towards the back with the tinkle of broken glass still in his ears.

Sam and Jim were waiting for him. They had mounted and Jim was holding his rein. Their faces shone. Jim cried, "Where to, partner?"

Bill said, "The shortest way to the TV. And go like hell. There'll be nobody there. It's the chance I've been looking for."

CHAPTER TWENTY

THEY RODE HARD, Sam and Jimmy still wearing their handcuffs. Bill knew that pursuit would begin within a matter of minutes, as soon as the crowd in the store could fight their way to their horses and get under way.

The first task of the fugitives was to try to throw their pursuers off the track; Bill needed time to go over the TV, for there was the possibility that there he would find some evidence which would connect Cleve Morley with the rustling. For the present they must continue straight onward; they were on open range and any change of course would be noticed at once. About a mile from the town the range became rolling, each successive rise looming higher as the hills drew nearer.

Bill shouted to the two ahead of him, "Any chance of throwing them off the trail? Delaying them?"

Jim called back, "Not until we get into the hills. Once there we can show 'em a trick or two."

So they kept on, their horses running full out, and if they did not gain on their pursuers Bill was sure the pursuers would not gain on them.

They entered the timber belt at last and slowed down for the steady climb. They were following the regular trail to the TV; to leave it meant slower progress and loss of what lead they had. As it was, Morley's men would cut down the distance between them because of their enforced reduction in speed.

They came at last to a mountain stream, forded it and rode for some distance along the trail, then, at Sam's suggestion, Bill cut off to his right with instructions to circle for half a mile and come to the stream higher up. A hundred yards farther, Jim left the trail, and finally Sam swung off to make his circle. Each entered the creek and turned upstream, met about a mile from where the trail crossed, then headed again for the TV. They hoped this maneuver would delay their pursuers for some time, especially since dusk would have fallen before they had ferreted out all three trails.

They made all speed for the twin valleys and at last sighted the buildings of Ed Thayer below them. They appeared deserted, as did those of the TV at the base of the mountain spur. They angled down to Thayer's range and headed for the TV. Darkness was gathering.

Sam led them to the gate in the fence which separated Morley's range from the ET, they passed through it and headed for the buildings. They rode swiftly, desiring to get under cover before their pursuers could sight them from the higher ground they had just left.

The ranch buildings were silent and empty and they circled a barn and tied their horses behind it. Bill tried his handcuff key on the manacles Sam and Jimmy wore but it would not unlock them. He said, "Go to the blacksmith shop and cut them off. Then look around for weapons; there must be rifles and extra sixguns in the bunkhouse. And keep out of sight."

They departed at a run and he entered the ranch house by the back door. He went through the kitchen and into another room which evidently served as an office, for there was a small safe and a roll-top desk in it. Bill's heart sank when he tried to twist the handle of the safe. It was locked.

He turned to the desk. This too was locked, but presented no problem. He pried the top open with his knife and rolled it back. He searched the pigeonholes, finding letters, bills for equipment, memos of various sorts. It was too dark to read, so he lighted the lamp which stood on the top of the desk and went through the papers quickly. There was nothing in them that even hinted at anything irregular in the conduct of the ranch. He started on the desk drawers.

These were a mess, containing everything from cigarette papers to fishing tackle. It took time to paw through them, and he did it systematically, beginning at the top drawer and working down on both sides. At first he had been conscious of the distant clang of a hammer, but now that had ceased and he guessed that Sam and Jimmy had freed themselves of their manacles.

And then he heard hoofbeats, a steady muted roll. He snapped erect. They must have seen the glow from the lamp, but it was too late to correct that now.

Jim came running into the room. "They're comin', Bill! We got to get out of here!" He was carrying a Winchester and had a Colt sixgun stuck behind the waistband of his levis. Bill looked regretfully at the safe, then yanked out the last of the desk drawers. Books! Tally books, a day book, ledgers! He grunted in satisfaction as he lifted them out. The hoofbeats were louder; he tucked the books under an arm and said, "Let's go."

They ran out through the kitchen, rounded the barn and found Sam waiting with the horses. They leaped into their saddles, Bill still clinging to the books. Sam asked, "Up the slope to the top of the spur?"

Bill said, "No. What we need is distance and we can get it as long as they're riding full out and can't hear us for their own noise. Along the bottom of the spur and into one of the valleys. We can climb out later."

They left at a gallop, skirting the bottom of the abruptly rising spur, following its contour into the west valley. The mountain shielded them with its blackness, preventing their pursuers seeing them. Three miles up the valley they halted to listen. Morley's men were still following them.

"Heard us when they stopped at the ranch," said Sam. "Bill, we sure are in a jam. We ain't got much lead and the spur is too steep-sided for us to climb it with hosses. We could do it afoot, but if we leave the hosses we're licked."

"There's a gap in the hills to the west," said Jimmy tightly. "We might make that."

"They'd hear us cutting across the valley and head us off," vetoed Bill. "No, we'll keep going straight ahead. If you see a clump of trees or brush big enough to hide us, head for it. They might over-run us and we can double back."

They rode on anxiously, their eyes stabbing at the dark sides of the spur in search of suitable cover. It was Bill who saw the dark mass of trees clustered in a little indentation in the mountain, and he called to the others and swerved his horse towards it.

The ground beneath them abruptly levelled out and they passed through a cut in a transverse ridge and into a tangle of second-growth. Trees suddenly loomed on both sides of them, but the ground remained level and they seemed to be on a beaten road. And then they came to a barrier of brush against the side of the mountain and reined to a halt.

"This'll have to do," said Bill tightly. They could hear the drum of hoofs out on the range. "If they follow us here, we'll have to make a break for it. Unless——" he twisted to peer at the brush barrier—"we can get behind that."

He urged his horse closer, tentatively grasped a dead limb and pulled. The limb came away. He said, "Lend a hand, you fellows. If we can pull out a few more branches we might be able to get behind it."

A passage wide enough for a horse was quickly cleared and Bill urged his mount through the opening. The animal shied at first, then moved ahead confidently. The stars were blotted out, but still the horse kept going. Bill turned in his saddle and saw the dark shapes of Sam and Jimmy following him; and beyond them he could see a dark archway limned against the starlit sky. He pulled up, said, "This seems to be a cave. We could hold them off forever if we had grub and water."

They sat their horses listening. The hoofbeats became a thunderous roll, then gradually receded in the distance. "They passed us," said Jimmy. "Now we can backtrack."

Bill said, "Wait a minute. Let's see how far this thing runs." He pushed on and they rode for another hundred feet. Once more they halted and Bill said, "This is no cave; this is a tunnel."

"Say!" exclaimed Sam. "I remember hearin' from somebody that years ago there used to be a big mine on the other side of east valley, and that some railroad run a spur through the west gap and over to it. Seems like I heard that they ran a tunnel through this spur to save goin' around it."

"Yeah?" Bill was tense.

"Sure they did! But it was a long time ago and when the mine petered out they tore up the tracks. You reckon this it it?"

"I sure do. That level stretch we hit was the old roadbed; the cut in that ridge was man-made. That means we can go right through and come out in the other valley."

"Wonder why Morley keeps the tunnel blocked up and never says nothin' about it?" said Jim. "You'd think he'd use it to push cattle from one valley to the other, wouldn't you?"

It came to Bill then. "Yes, you would. You'd think just that. And that's just what he does do. Boys, the man we want for this rustling is Cleve Morley!"

"Morley!" exclaimed Sam in unbelief. "How you figger that?"

"I'll bet my hat against a chaw of tobacco that Morley doesn't run more than five thousand head of cattle. Never has. And five thousand head won't furnish the two thousand a year to fill his Government contracts."

"You said you tallied his cattle yourself," reminded Jim.

"I did. Spent a day in the west valley tallying them and counted just about five thousand. The crew bunched them right against this hill while we tallied. And when we'd finished I rode back to the ranch house with the foreman and bedded down for the night. And the next day we went into the east valley and counted five thousand head. Five thousand added to five thousand makes ten thousand in any man's arithmetic. Only trouble was, I counted the same five thousand twice; for while I was bedded down for the night the crew pushed the whole bunch through this tunnel and into the east valley."

"Good gosh and the cows come home!" almost whispered Jimmy. "Prove that, Bill, and you got Morley's hide nailed to the barn!"

"I reckon," said Sam in a voice which said he fully expected to be disappointed, "we'd better make sure first that this tunnel runs clear through."

"You're right," said Bill, and once more sent his horse ahead.

They moved on for several hundred yards, then Bill suddenly halted and said in a low voice. "Listen!"

They sat their horses in silence and presently there came to them the soft *plop, plop* of hoofs. The sounds came from some point ahead of them, not behind them. Bill whispered, "Hold everything!"

The hoofbeats grew louder, echoing in the enclosed space. And then they abruptly ceased and a man's voice reached them, loud in the stillness. "Reckon it's safe to start a fire? There's somethin' goin' on in the west valley sure as hell."

"Safe enough," came the answer. "Hell! Who's gonna see any fire in here with both ends blocked? I'm fed up with the dark; I'm sick and tired of livin' like a prairie dog."

"Well, you strip the hosses and I'll start her up. Like livin' in a stable with them hosses beddin' down in here."

"And I'm gettin' all smoked up," complained the other. "But we got to have a fire. Get her goin'."

Came sundry sounds—the cracking of sticks, the squeak of leather, the grumbled oaths of the man who was off-saddling in the darkness, the impatient stamp of hoofs. Bill put out his hand, found Sam's arm and squeezed it; then slipped his right leg carefully over the saddle and lowered himself soundlessly to the ground.

Sam passed the signal on to Jim and did likewise. Jim followed and the three stood half-crouched beside their horses. Bill drew his Colt and moved silently forward and they followed. He saw a flicker of light near the ground then a blaze as the dry wood caught. A man was fanning the flames with his hat. The man was dark and smooth-shaven. Just within the circle of light another man was pulling the saddle off the second horse. He dropped the rig and led both horses along the tunnel. The fire blazed higher and the dark-haired man put his hat on his head.

The second man came slouching along out of the blackness and up to the fire. He stood spraddle-legged before it and started to roll a cigarette. He was big and red-haired and freckle-faced.

One of the advancing men struck a stone with his foot and it gave a little clatter. The dark man snapped a startled face towards them; the redhead dropped tobacco and paper and reached for his gun.

"Don't try it, Harrington!" snapped Bill.

But Harrington had gone too far to stop; his Colt whipped up, there was the blended thunder of three guns and as many lead slugs ripped through his body. He went down like a ton of bricks.

Harvey Short stood with his arms extended as though he were trying to raise the mountain. His eyes were wide and startled. The three moved towards him, their guns still levelled and smoking. Bill reached out and plucked the fellow's Colt from its holster and tossed it to one side.

Bill still had the TV ranch books under his left arm. He said, "You can take 'em down now and relax, Harvey. You can even sit down. That's a right nice fire and by its light we're going to audit the books of Cleve Morley's ranch. And then you and me are going to have a talk. Or you'll talk and I'll listen."

"I—I don't know nothin'!"

"That's just too bad. For I'm going to finish up this mess tonight and if I have to finish you in the process I won't mind it a bit. Not—one—damned—bit."

CHAPTER TWENTY-ONE

FOR A WHILE after Bill had gone, Pat lay looking up at the shelter ceiling. She was thinking of Bill, of his big, clean body and the strong face that he always managed to keep freshly shaved, of the slightly cynical twist of his lips and the stern, cold eyes that had unexpectedly warmed as he looked down at her.

She had come very, very close to returning his kiss, and she was a bit amazed at herself. The impulse to meet his lips had been as natural as to take an offered hand, and only remembrance of her biting words to him that day in the cabin had enabled her to turn her head at the last moment.

He wanted her and he had told her that he intended to have her. But he would not take her against her will. Just like the kiss; willingly or not at all. Not like Cleve Morley.

Thought of Morley brought a moment of panic. He must have been furious when he arrived at the cabin to find her gone. He had promised to hang her father and Jimmy if she failed to meet him there and he would surely keep that promise if he possibly could. But Bill had assured her that they would not hang and Bill was stronger in every way than Morley could ever hope to be. The knowledge comforted her and she got off the bunk with a suddenly discovered appetite.

She was stiff and sore, for she had not ridden much recently; but she knew from experience that she must keep moving. She put beans and bacon on a tin plate and walked about the shelter while she ate. Then she filled a cup with strong coffee and sipped at it, still pacing.

Now that she was moving, she decided to make a real walk of it. She went outside and climbed the slope and entered the fringe of trees. Her mind was active as she strode along, automatically following the trail they had made. Bill would save them provided he reached Pandora in time. But suppose something happened to him? His horse was tired and he would force it; suppose it stepped into a hole and broke its leg? Well, there was her horse; he had taken it along and could use it.

But had he taken it along? She decided that he hadn't. Not very far, at any rate. He would not want to be hampered with a led horse; he'd park the animal somewhere sufficiently distant from the claim. He had told her to wait here and she experienced a little thrill of pleasure at his fear for her safety. A man like Bill wouldn't show so much concern over a girl he simply wanted to—to sleep with. There must be some deeper emotion, some nobler one. Perhaps——! She felt her cheeks warm and pushed the thought from her mind.

How would she pass the time while awaiting his return, torn by uncertainty and doubt and tortured by the thought that perhaps he had failed to save them? He couldn't possibly return before the morrow. Maybe the day after. Maybe even later. And all the while—!

She stopped suddenly, stood staring. She had come farther than she had thought and now she found herself gazing at something in a little patch of grass by a small mountain stream. It was her horse! It was grazing and she could see the hobbled feet. Suddenly, she knew that her problem had been solved for her. She would return to Pandora. If Bill had freed her father and brother she would keep out of Morley's sight; if he hadn't, she'd explain to Cleve that Bill had forced her to go with him and perhaps he'd be willing to go through with their bargain.

She looked for her saddle and bridle, found them in a clump of brush and, taking the latter with her, walked down to the horse. When she had adjusted the bridle she dropped the rein and the horse stood while she removed the hobbles. She cinched on the saddle, mounted and set out for Pandora.

She was stiff and sore, but she gritted her teeth and put the horse to a fast pace. When noon came she halted only long enough to rest her mount and water him sparingly. She was uncertain of the way back and now the trail she followed was not familiar to her. She rode on, becoming more confused by the mile and finally found herself on rough terrain that she knew she had not traversed before. A little later she realized that she was hopelessly lost.

She moaned in despair; she couldn't afford to lose time. In desperation she finally let the horse have his head in the hope that he would be able to find his way home.

He did, but dusk had fallen by the time she recognized a landmark and it was quite dark when they emerged in the basin where the cabin was located. The horse wanted to stop, but she spurred him on towards Pandora. It was after ten o'clock when she entered the town.

She did not ride down the street, but reined into an alley and dismounted behind some dark buildings. She tied the horse and stole up a passageway to the street. It was dark and as far as she could see deserted, but the saloons were lighted and the sound of voices drifted to her. She had to ask somebody about her father and brother and thought first of the Widow Wilkins. She decided that it was unlikely that Mrs. Wilkins knew and remembered the dark-haired girl at the Silver Saddle. Perhaps she could locate her from the doorway of the place and call to her.

She started for the Silver Saddle, keeping to the shadows.

THERE was an air of repressed excitement in the Silver Saddle that night. Men gathered in knots at the bar or around the gaming tables, discussing the events of the late afternoon, reviewing again the scene in the improvised courtroom when Bill Serviss had entered at the window and had departed again with the prisoners.

They discussed Bill in tones of admiration. Pink Paradine was not well liked and the quick polishing off of the marshal was a morsel to be chewed thoughtfully and digested appreciatively. And Bill's blunt accusation that Cleve Morley had tried to buy the Larkin girl with her father's and brother's freedom had shocked them. Cleve was supposed to be a gentleman. They knew of his liaison with Gloria and accepted it with equanimity; Gloria was a girl whose business it was to dole out favors for a consideration. They found no fault with the bargains she made or the ones who did the purchasing.

But Pat Larkin was different. She was a good kid and only a low-down skunk would use his power to force her to sleep with him. Might just as well chloroform her and take her then. The furtive glances which were tossed in Cleve's direction held distaste and disapproval.

Cleve took the looks standing up. He was at his end of the bar, chewing on a dead cigar, his face impassive, only the restlessness of his eyes telling of the rage which burned within him. He had been publicly humiliated; not only had his prisoners been taken from him but also he had been branded a libertine and a would-be thief of virtue. Being a gentleman, that hurt.

Even Gloria had spat at him in the courtroom. Right in public. Goddam her, he'd have her hide for that! He glanced over at a corner where she sat with a glass of whiskey for company. She was mad and surly and no man had approached her. They were almost as afraid of her as they were of Morley.

Cleve brazened it out, hoping for word from his men that they had caught up with Bill and the escaped prisoners. Jigger Malone, the TV foreman, would not fall down on the job, he was sure. A thorough chap, Malone. And it didn't seem possible that the three could get away clean. Some of Ed Thayer's men had joined in the chase and there were enough of them to blast Serviss and the Larkins clear out of their boots. But no word came from the fighting front and Cleve began to get restless.

By ten o'clock he could endure it no longer. The lowvoiced conversation, the shaking heads, the sidelong glances were getting under his skin. He did not dare show it. He yawned and looked casually around. The girls were idle, and Maybelle was seated at the blackjack table dealing out cards and then gathering them together again. Cleve strolled over, watched for a moment then said, "I don't believe I know that game."

She answered without looking up, her voice moody. "It's not solitaire. I'm tellin' my fortune. See that Ace of Spades that keeps turnin' up? That's the death card."

"If it was Serviss's fortune, I'd cheer," he said gloomily and walked on.

Damn Serviss! How had he got word of the appointment with Pat? She'd told him, of course. He'd probably ridden out there to have some more of the same and had found her waiting for Cleve. And she had gone away with him. A lot her father and brother meant to her compared with Bill Serviss! His anger burning even hotter, he went outside and mounted the covered stairs and entered his room.

He lighted a lamp, tossed his hat onto a chair, stretched out on the bed and locked his hands behind his head. He heard heel-taps in the hall and made a grimace of distaste. Sounded like Gloria. Damn her! Why hadn't he locked the door?

She came in without knocking; just pushed open the door and strode in. Her face was flushed and her eyes glinted. She came over to the bed and glared down at him. "You son of a bitch! So it's been the Larkin girl the whole time?"

He was thoroughly fed up with her. "You finally tumbled, eh? Sure it's the Larkin girl. She was to wait for me last night on the homestead. Who tipped Serviss off to it, you?" He knew she hadn't but he wanted to hurt her.

"If I'd known it I'd have cut her heart out!"

"Don't tell me I mean that much to you. You'll get along without me. You still have Bill. Or has he given you the brush-off, too?"

"No man gives me the brush-off and gets away with it!" she said hotly.

He lay on the bed gazing up at her. She was wearing a low-cut dress and if she had a weapon on her person she could not get to it in a hurry. He said, "I seem to be getting away with it. You're through, baby. This is your last night at the Silver Saddle; better make arrangements with somebody for your bed and board."

"You just think you're getting away with it! I'm not through, but you are!"

She stooped, snatched at the hem of her dress and lifted the garment. Her right hand gripped the knife she had run through her garter and drew it. There was too much to do and too short a time to do it in; Cleve was off the bed as she raised the thin-bladed knife and had her by the wrist before she could strike.

He twisted savagely and she screamed in rage and pain but clung to the knife. She tried to pull her arm free and the pull was instinctively downward. The point of the knife was towards her and Cleve pushed slightly on her arm. The sharp blade ripped into her cheek and cut a gash from the corner of the eye to the chin. She screamed horribly and dropped the knife and Cleve kicked it into a corner.

He stepped back a pace to observe her, a bit upset at the consequence of their struggle; then salved his conscience by reminding himself that he was not to blame and spoke harshly. "You damned fool, you ought to know better than to try a trick like that with me! Get over to the doctor and have him sew that up for you. Here." He snatched a towel from the washstand and pushed it into her hands. The blood was streaming from the cut and dripping from her chin.

She held the cloth to her face, her eyes wide and startled, rooted to the floor with pain and shock. He took her arm and turned her and walked her to the doorway and thrust her through it. "Get over to the doctor's and get that fixed before you bleed all over the place." She started down the hall staggering slightly; then she moved faster and her heels clicked hysterically as she ran down the steps.

Morley went back into the room and looked about him. There were a few bloodstains on the floor and he got another towel and wiped them away, then kicked the towel out of sight beneath the wash-stand. He was sweating. He walked to a window and stared out into the night, and suddenly he needed air. He picked up his hat and went out, leaving the light burning.

The excitement caused by the struggle and the shock of seeing the open wound passed quickly and he was aware of a little feeling of satisfaction. That cut would leave a scar that would forever mar the beauty of Gloria Gale. Served her right; she had made enough trouble. Maybe now she'd have to find a decent way of making a living. Perhaps he had done her soul a favor. He grinned mirthlessly at the thought that she might have a soul and stepped into the alley.

He stood there for a few minutes, breathing deeply, then turned and walked along the passageway beside the saloon and towards the street. He reached the dark front corner and was about to turn it when a shadowy form came quickly into the passageway and bumped squarely into him.

Instinctively, he put his arms out to ward off the other. There came a startled exclamation and his eyes blazed and his arms closed around a soft body. "Well!" he said softly; and then again, *"Well!"*

Pat had cut across the street and moved directly to the front of the Silver Saddle, dodging the weak light which filtered through a front window and stooping so as to be in the shadow of the half-doors. She listened for a moment to the voices, then parted the doors slightly and peered through the crack.

She looked first for Cleve Morley and gave a little sigh of thanksgiving when she saw he was not in the room. She sent her gaze about in search of the dark-haired girl and saw her sitting at a table in the rear of the room studying some cards which lay before her. She was out of reach of Pat's voice and Pat shrank from entering the place. She looked beyond Maybelle and saw the back door; she could call to Maybelle from there and not be heard by anyone else because of the noise.

She let the doors fall gently into place, moved away and turned towards the passageway which led to the alley. She ran lightly, anxious to reach the door before Maybelle moved away from the table. She rounded the dark corner, saw a vague figure loom up before her and bumped solidly into it. She gave a little exclamation and was about to draw back, but arms went about her and the man spoke and she knew it was Cleve Morley.

She said, "Let me go."

"Why? I like you this way. Where were you last night? We had an appointment, you know."

She said quickly, "My father—Jimmy! Where are they?"

His wits were as nimble as ever. She did not know! He said, "Where do you think they are?"

He heard her gasp. "You—didn't——?"

"Hang them? Not yet. I decided to give you a little grace. When I found you gone and the lamp still burning I decided that somebody, Bill Serviss probably, had forced you to leave. Was I right?"

"Yes! Yes, he did! Somehow he'd heard of—of our appointment. He made me go with him to a place in the hills and he left me there. He started back for town——" Apprehension gripped her. "Where is he?"

Morley laughed lightly. She didn't know where Bill was, either. Things were coming his way with a rush. He said, "He's safe. With the other two. He shot Pink Paradine and that's murder, you know. I think we'll hang three instead of two."

It seemed to Pat that her heart had stopped beating. So Bill had tried to save them and had been captured in the attempt. And he had killed Pandora's marshal. All because of her. She said weakly, "Oh, no!"

He sighed, sadly. "I'm afraid so. Unless——Well, I might be persuaded to be lenient. I might even be persuaded to arrange a jail break."

She grasped eagerly at the offer, pride and shame entirely gone. "Oh, please, Cleve! I'll go with you anywhere—do anything!"

"That sounds nice." He was purring now. He drew her to him, kissed her hair, her eyes; then straightened abruptly at the thought that they might be interrupted here and that once more he would be forced to relinquish this precious prize. He released her and gripped her by the wrist. "This way," he said, and drew her after him along the passageway. She followed.

They rounded the rear corner and he nodded towards the door to the covered stairway. "I have the nicest little room," he told her softly. "If I had known I was going to meet you I would have had it cleaned up a bit, but I think you'll like it." He opened the door, released her wrist, made a little bow. "After you, my darling. Straight along the hall. The last door on the right."

He followed her up, closing the door behind him. He hadn't noticed the figure sitting dejectedly on the back steps of the saloon just six feet away. It was dark and he had eyes for nothing but this delicious girl who was going so willingly to his room.

The figure erected itself and Maybelle said in a choked voice, "My God!" She stood for a moment thinking, trying to find a way to save Pat from this beast. The only one she could think of was Bill. But he had fled with the two Larkins. There was just a chance——

She ran along the passageway to the street and turned left. Her high heels clicked on the plank sidewalk as she sped towards the place where he always made his camp.

CHAPTER TWENTY-TWO

HARVEY SHORT TALKED. He talked plenty and willingly. He talked because even his dumb wits could grasp the fact that Morley was sunk even without a confession on his part.

Bill had studied the books by the light of the fire and their contents had been revealing. They would not have been so revealing to one who was not suspicious, who did not know what to look for. The revealing things were dates of delivery and brands. If Morley had delivered from his own herd all the cattle would have borne the TV brand; but there were references to Window Sash and Box Cross brands and also a few Cinchbuckles. And at least one of the delivery dates was very significant.

Five days after the theft of the fifty ET steers the day book recorded the delivery of fifty Window Sash steers. Well, add a couple straight lines to the ET brand and you would have a Window Sash. When he had read this entry Bill glanced up at Short and said, "You fellers took quite a chance delivering those Window Sash steers before the brands had healed, didn't you?"

Short said, "No," then checked himself, put on a blank look and said, "Huh?"

"Don't be backward about coming forward," said Bill. "You're going to talk even if I have to heat that running iron we found on your saddle and do a little fancy branding of my own. You'd look sort of nice with a bit T right in the middle of your forehead."

Short licked his lips and said nothing.

"I asked a question," said Bill harshly. "I asked if you didn't take a chance delivering those steers before the worked-over brands had healed."

Short said, "We'd delivered Window Sashes before. Gover'ment ain't too partic'lar about brands; all they want is beef."

"After the TV crew rustled those steers they turned 'em over to you and Texas and Swat and Paradine and you drove them north, knowing I'd think they were headed towards the border. You added those lines with a running iron and then hurried them right along and gave a bill of sale for fifty head of Window Sash steers, didn't you?"

Short said nothing.

"Jim," said Bill impatiently, "we haven't any time to waste. Get that running iron off the saddle and put it in the fire, will you?"

Jim got the iron and poked it into the fire and Bill continued to study the day book. After a while he said, "Here's an interesting item: 'Harrington, Texas, Short and Paradine, for services on drive, two hundred dollars.' Fifty bucks apiece, huh? Cleve cleans up two thousand and gives you boys two hundred. Pretty cheap, I'd say.... That iron red yet, Jim?"

Jim examined it. "Just about."

Bill said, "It'll do, Won't burn so fast, but it'll do."

Short said, "What do you want to know?"

Bill regarded him steadily. "Everything. And this is your last chance. I'll take it down in writing and you can sign it when you're through."

"And—what do I get out of it?"

"That's up to the judge. Come clean and I'll put in a good word for you."

So Harvey Short came clean. He had nothing to lose; Morley was done in any event. Those entries in the books would convict him, especially if Bill checked back with Government on the freshness of those Window Sash brands. Once committed, Short talked willingly enough. Bill had been right; Morley owned about five thousand head, not ten. The extra steers he needed to fill his contract were rustled from neighboring ranchers. Brands were altered where it was possible and the animals were held until the scars had healed. Except in this last instance, when delivery had been postponed and the animals were needed in a hurry.

Yes, they had rustled some Candlesticks—it was so easy to change the brands to a Cinchbuckle—but Cole Brent had started getting tough. Short didn't know whether Brent suspected Morley, but they didn't dare push him too far. The whole TV crew were in on it; they picked up the stock and passed it along to the other four. When the deliveries were large, the crew helped to drive. In those cases there were enough TV cattle to hide the others.

The abandoned railroad tunnel had been forgotten years ago, but Morley had seen that he could use it to conceal the real number of cattle he ran. The fence kept Ed Thayer's cattle off TV range and they did not have to worry about some rep from the ET finding the tunnel and guessing what it was used for. Nobody suspected Cleve Morley, president of the Cattlemen's Association.

Bill summarized the statement, wrote it down and had Short sign it. He said, "One thing we forgot. That hide found in Sam's lean-to. You had to destroy that sick steer and Cleve caught up with you and you dug up the remains and gave it to him, didn't you?"

"Not me. Texas. We'd kept the beef and had buried the hide and head and entrails and legs."

"Remember that. We don't need it, but it's nice to know." He turned to the two Larkins. "Sam, you and Jim escort Harvey to Cole Brent's ranch. You may be able to head him off before he gets there; he was in town when we left and I don't reckon he traveled quite as fast. Tell him what happened. Tell him to take his crew and round up the TV outfit and bring them to the jail in Pandora. I'm going there now and take over. If Ed Thayer is still in town I'll get him to help me. But I figure I won't need too much help. Morley should be smart enough to know when he's licked. We'll go out the tunnel into east valley.

They saddled Short's pony and tied him to the saddle and left Swat Harrington's body lying where it was. They hazed the extra horse before them and turned it loose on the range. The Larkins headed for the trail which led to Brent's ranch and Bill struck out for town.

It was shortly after ten when he entered Pandora and he did not ride at once to his usual camping place as had been his custom. He rode straight to the Silver Saddle and dismounted outside it. He heard the click of heels on the sidewalk and knew from the sound that a woman was running up the street, but this did not concern him.

He walked to the swinging doors of the saloon and looked over them. Morley was not in the room, nor were Gloria and Maybelle. He heard again the quick tap of heels and turned. The thin light from the window fell across the face of a girl. It was a worried face, with glittering eyes and the hair that framed it was dark. He stepped forward to meet her and said, "Maybelle!"

"Bill!" The word was a prayer of thanks. "Oh, Bill! Morley just took Pat Larkin up to his room!"

"Pat Larkin! You're loco, cow gal. I left Pat Larkin miles away from here; a full day's ride."

"I'm not loco!" She was shaking his arm as though to awaken him. "I tell you I saw her, heard her! She mustn't know her father and brother escaped. I tell you she went upstairs with him! I started for your camp, then turned and recognized you by the light from the doors. Bill, hurry!"

There was no doubt about it now. Somehow, Pat had found her horse and had come back; and, not knowing that he had gotten away with Sam and Jim, she had offered to keep her bargain with Morley. He cursed harshly, pushed past Maybelle and started for the alley at a run. He took the steps two at a time, ran along the hall to the last door on the right and turned the knob. The door was locked.

"Who is it?" came Morley's voice from within. The voice was impatient, angry.

"Serviss! Open up or I'll break the door down."

There was a moment of silence; then, "I don't think you'd better try it, Serviss. I'm armed and you're wanted for murder. I can kill you before you get your balance and it'll be a pleasure, I assure you!"

"Morley, I'm coming in. I want you; I've got the goods on you. Harvey Short talked and I have his signed confession. Also I have the TV books and know all about the Window Sash brand. And I've got men posted around the place. You can't get away."

He heard a little cry in a girl's voice, quickly suppressed. He cried, "Pat, you there?"

Morley answered. "Yes, she's in here. It looks as though she might be my ticket to safety. If I were you I'd think twice about breaking in. I'd be sure to get you, and then, if there's no other way out, I could shoot her, too."

A spasm of apprehension shook Bill. "Even you are not dog enough to do that, Morley! They'd tear you apart."

"If they get the chance. I'd have to risk it." Morley's voice was pitched higher than was normal, as though hysteria had crept in.

Bill said tightly, "Pat, you all right?"

Again the answer came from Morley. "Yes, she's all right—so far. She isn't talking because I have my gun pointed at her. She'll continue to be all right if you see reason."

"What do you mean by that?" Bill was temporizing for the first time in his life. Maybelle had stooped over and was trying to look through the keyhole.

He heard the pad of footsteps as Morley approached the door. Cleve lowered his voice in a tense whisper. "Serviss, you alone out there?"

"Yes."

"Let me go and she's all yours. I swear it! I haven't touched her. I'll come out with her in front of me and you drop your gun and turn your face to the wall. I have a key to Gloria's room. I'll take Pat in there with me and lock the door. From the window I can get onto the roof of the next building. I know my way from there; I can get clear by the time you break in. She'll be there, waiting for you. Is it a deal?"

Gone was all sense of duty, all thoughts of anything but Pat's safety. Bill opened his lips to cry yes when there came the sound of a furious struggle. Pat's voice rose in a scream. *"Bill! Bill!"*

Maybelle came to her feet. "She jumped him! Bust in that damned door!"

Bill leaped to the opposite wall, braced his foot against it and hurled his hard body at the door. He hit it with every ounce of strength and power that his seasoned muscles and the momentum could furnish. It splintered under the impact like matchwood; the upper hinge was torn loose and he fell into the room after it. The bottom, flapping out on a twisted hinge, tripped him as though he had run against a stretched rope; he went sprawling flat on his stomach atop the wrecked door and the force of the fall tore the gun from his hand.

He had a fleeting glimpse of the scene before his agonized eyes. Pat had been clinging to Morley's gun arm, and he had just flung her from him. She was staggering backwards, toppling, her fingers still clawed as they had been when shaken free. And Morley, his face a tight, furious mask, was bringing the gun around. It steadied, the muzzle pointed at Bill's staring face, and he saw the spasmodic twitch of the face muscles as Morley squeezed the trigger.

And then something was sprawling over him, a tangle of soft flesh and silky garments, and the gun was blotted out an instant before it roared. He gasped, "Good God! Maybelle, Maybelle!" and heard her cry. "Joe! Joe!" The body on his went limp and the head dropped and strands of dark hair dangled before his face. Through it he could see Morley's feet dancing around as the man shifted position trying to find an angle where he could put a bullet into Bill.

From the doorway behind Bill came a thunderous report and the feet gave one more convulsive leap and then the legs began to bend. Bill saw Morley's knees come into sight, then his hips. His arms dangled lifelessly, the fingers went lax and the gun dropped to the floor. Then Morley plunged downward, rolled over, kicked one leg and lay still.

And behind and above Bill came Gloria's voice, so harsh and thick that he could hardly recognize it. "I told you you were through, you bastard!"

CHAPTER TWENTY-THREE

Bill wiggled gently from beneath Maybelle's limp body, got to his knees and turned her on her back. She was dead, the bullet having gone into the top of her head. The dark hair concealed the horror of the wound. Bill's mouth was working and there were angry tears in his eyes. He said brokenly, "You poor kid! You poor, dear kid!"

The dead face looked up at him and he saw it was tranquil. There was even the hint of a smile on the red lips and the glad look in the dark eyes had not yet been erased. She was with her Joe at last and she was happy.

He looked towards Pat. She was sitting on the floor where she had fallen, bracing herself with her arms, and the shock and fear in the dark eyes went out slowly and he saw infinite gladness come into them. She said in a whisper, "Bill! You're safe! Oh, thank God!"

"And Maybelle," he said huskily. "Don't forget her."

He looked once more into Maybelle's face and saw that the eyes had glazed over now. He turned his head slowly and looked through the doorway. Gloria was standing there, and the shotgun in her hands still eddied smoke. A bandage covered the right side of her face and her eyes still blazed.

Even as he watched, the fury which had distorted her face left and the smooth left cheek went soft again and the eyes lost their cold, hard brilliance and became once more limpid and infinitely sad. She was looking at Cleve. She stood looking for half a minute, then her shoulders sagged, the shotgun dropped from her fingers. She turned slowly and walked across the hall to her room, and suddenly she had become an old woman.

In their excitement they had not been aware of the thunder of hoofs in the street, the cries of men, the furious pound of boots on the back stairs. Now men swarmed into the room, fierce-eyed men with guns in their hands. In the lead was Cole Brent and behind him were Sam and Jim Larkin. They halted abruptly inside the doorway, looking about in shock and bewilderment.

Bill heard Pat's glad cry, "Dad! Jimmy!" and saw her spring to her feet as they ran towards her.

Brent said, "What in hell happened here, Serviss?"

He told them. And as he talked, the noise in the hallway subsided as men crowded about to listen. On the far side of the room, Pat and Sam and Jim had finished their greetings and were listening, too.

When he had finished, Cole Brent looked down at the dead Maybelle and slowly removed his hat. He cleared his throat. "Fellers, there lays a real lady! God rest her soul!"

And Bill said gravely, "Amen!"

There wasn't much more left for them to do. Sam and Jim had intercepted Brent and the Candlestick crew on the home trail and Brent had not waited to gather in the TV crew. Apprehensive for Bill's safety, they had headed straight for town. They had fetched Short with them and he was still roped to his saddle and under guard. They left almost at once for the TV to finish the job, and Thayer and some of his men who had remained in town went with them. There would be a grand roundup that night!

Texas Tom was dead; so were Swat Harrington and Pink Paradine. Morley was dead. Gloria was done in Pandora and Maybelle had gone to join her Joe. Sam and Jimmy Larkin were freed of the stigma of cattle rustling and Sam had shed the weight of years of hard luck from his shoulders. He stood erect and the beaten look had left his eyes. He was almost cheerful. Jimmy bubbled over with excitement and happiness. He was going to ride the claim the next morning and Sam was going to the county seat to file on it.

They told Pat about it on the ride to the Larkin homestead, waiting until they were out on the open range where there was no danger of being overheard. Bill, who rode beside Pat, confirmed their report as to the richness of the claim. They could have everything they wanted now.

They rode in a compact bunch at first, but when they had passed on the good news, Sam and Jim took the lead and Bill rode behind with Pat. Their stirrups touched and Bill was holding her hand. A week or two earlier he would have blushed with shame to know that he was acting like a school kid with his first sweetheart.

Well, he was a schoolboy and he was just beginning to learn about women. Pat's kind, that is. He knew now that Maybelle had been right when she said there were decent women in the world. And Pat *was* his first sweetheart.

They didn't say much, and they rode slowly so that by the time they reached the cabin Sam and Jim were in their bunks snoring. They had left a light burning in the kitchen and when Bill would have said a reluctant goodnight, Pat shook her dusky head. "Not yet, Bill. Come in, please."

So, they tiptoed into the kitchen and Pat closed the door to the other room, and they sat down and looked across the room at each other, and again Pat saw warmth and tenderness in the eyes that could be so cold and hard.

She said, "It seems an awfully long time, doesn't it, since that first day when—when—?" She broke off, the pink climbing into her cheeks.

"When I walked out on you. I know now why I did that."

Her eyes were tender with the memory. "And you told me that some day I'd come yapping to you like a little dog."

Strangely enough, it was he who blushed now. And then he did something that brought wonder and puzzlement to her eyes. Solemnly he got down on all fours and came slowly across the floor to her. He was looking up at her and the hunger was in his eyes again. He stopped at her feet and slowly raised to his haunches, his hands dangling like paws. He looked at her and said, *"Yap, yap!"*

And then she knew. It was Bill who was coming yapping!

She laughed delightedly and there was a note of infinite tenderness in the laugh. She bent over impulsively and took his cheeks between her soft palms. The dark eyes were very soft and seductive. She bent forward and kissed him on the lips. "For a good doggie!" she whispered.

He gathered her into his arms and no longer was she stiff and frowning. Her lips sought his, clung to them. Her eyes were closed.

He said thickly, "When, darling? Oh, when?"

"Any time, Bill. Any time you say. Now, if you wish!"

He held her away from him and gazed into her eyes and saw only love and complete surrender. He took a deep breath. He shook his head. "No, darling; not that way. There's a parson in Pandora."

"Tomorrow, then."

"Tomorrow."

He gave a sudden start, leaped to his feet, the old Bill once more.

"Tomorrow? It *is* tomorrow—right now! Come on!" He dragged her to her feet, moved swiftly to the door, pulling her after him.

"But—Bill! Where?"

"To Pandora! To get that sky pilot out of bed!"

www.ingramcontent.com/pod-product-compliance
Lightning Source LLC
LaVergne TN
LVHW091149080826
845145LV00008B/2314

9781952138928